# CRYPTID ZOO

## GERRY GRIFFITHS

SEVERED PRESS
HOBART TASMANIA

# CRYPTID ZOO

*ISBN:* *978-1-925840-08-7*

*DEDICATION*

*For our wonderful Abbie,*
*You never cease to amaze us*

# 1

## NIGHT HUNT

Jack Tremens spotted a tiny white blip flash across the black screen on the instrument panel. "Did you see that?"

The pilot shook his head.

Jack turned around in the co-pilot's seat. Miguel Walla was leaning forward in the rear seat, staring intently at the screen. "It's not one of them."

"You sure?"

"It was running on all fours."

"Are we close?" Jack asked the pilot.

"We're just about there." The pilot pushed the yoke forward and they flew precariously low over the desert nightscape.

A minute later the skids touched down on the rock-covered sand.

Jack grabbed his gear, opened the side door, and climbed out. He waited until Miguel stepped down then signaled to the pilot.

The chopper lifted off and banked toward a butte where the pilot was instructed to wait for an hour before returning to pick them up unless Jack summoned him sooner with his miniature two-way radio tucked in his ear.

Once the helicopter was gone, the night around them became eerily quiet.

Jack pulled his watch cap down around his ears. "Why is it the desert can get so damn hot during the day and be so frigging cold at night?"

"Be happy we're not in the Gobi," Miguel said.

Jack thought back to their time in the Mongolian desert where they endured a week of sweltering heat trekking across the burning sand in search of an elusive specimen that dwelled underground.

One evening Jack and Miguel had stayed up late getting drunk on *Arkhi*, Mongolian vodka made from fermented cow milk yogurt, and later passed out in their tents.

Luckily, Jack's full bladder had gotten him up in the middle of the night. Stumbling out of his tent, he'd fallen facedown in six inches of snow. Jack rousted Miguel and they built a fire to stay warm as during the night the temperature had dropped to below freezing due to an extreme climate change.

It seemed ironic that a night of binge drinking would actually save their lives.

Jack and Miguel took a moment to put on their night vision goggles.

"Like being on another planet," Jack said, scanning the green imagery of flatland dotted with barrel cacti and scraggly shrubs.

"Full of crazy creatures," Miguel said.

"Yeah."

Both men wore side arms: Jack a Colt .44 Magnum revolver and Miguel, his .357 Desert Eagle semi-automatic pistol. They hoped they didn't need to use the weapons, as they had come specially outfitted to capture their intended prey alive.

Jack carried a Remington pump shotgun loaded with rubber dum dum bullets, which at a distance had adequate stopping power, but he knew at close range were still lethal so he had to be careful.

Miguel's weapon was a high-tech stun gun on a long pole with a battery pack and a regulated charge with a maximum of 200,000-volts.

"You know, Dr. McCabe said it doesn't matter whether it's dead or alive," Miguel said.

"I know what he said. But how do you properly replicate one of these things if you don't know what makes it tick?"

"You just want to impress Professor Howard."

"Maybe. So what if I do?"

"Just nice to know in case you get us both killed."

"No one's getting—" Jack paused and put his hand up to his ear. "It's the pilot. He's picking up targets, south of us. Maybe coyotes."

Miguel had his finger pressed on his earbud. "But not the four-legged kind."

They crouched and scampered for cover behind a large bush.

Jack peered between the branches with his night vision goggles and scanned the desert for anything that moved.

A thermal image of a man appeared, running across the rugged desert floor. He was wearing a backpack and carrying a plastic water jug. A woman came into view lugging a tote bag.

Soon there were more of them, all weighed down with rucksacks, each struggling to keep up with the rest of the illegal immigrants having crossed the border.

They looked like invading aliens in the green glow.

"Mules," Miguel whispered.

Jack counted three men with assault rifles—armed cartel thugs—wrangling the frightened people. He turned and looked at Miguel.

Miguel shook his head.

Even if they intervened, they were clearly outgunned. There was nothing Jack and Miguel could do but wait until they passed. Hopefully there wouldn't be another group right behind.

When the drug traffickers were far enough away, Jack pushed a button on his wristwatch and the crystal lit up. "We have forty-three minutes before our ride comes back." He looked at Miguel. "A case of Coronas if this works."

"It will." Miguel unzipped a duffle bag all the way. He reached inside, pulled out a small piñata shaped like a goat, and placed it on the ground.

"Weren't you supposed to send that for your daughter's birthday?"

"I was but Maria says Sophia is now into unicorns," Miguel said, reaching back into the bag. He took out an MP3 player and a plastic bottle. He handed the media device to Jack.

Jack had been skeptical when Miguel had first proposed the idea of using a dummy, but figured it was worth a shot. He knew they couldn't bring a real goat, as it would have cried the whole time once it sensed danger.

Besides, he'd seen what those things could do to a live animal and it was pretty gruesome.

Miguel unscrewed the cap off the plastic bottle and poured a thick liquid over the piñata. "The goat blood should draw them out."

"Time to set the trap." Jack placed the digital audio player on the ground under the cardboard goat then turned it on.

A distressed kid blatted for its mother from the tiny speaker.

Jack and Miguel snuck over to a nearby bush to wait.

It took only ten minutes for the ruse to work.

The creature that lurked out of the darkness was nearly four-feet tall and stood on two legs.

Fish eyes gaped from the egg-shaped head. Its mouth was open like a deep round bowl, revealing needle-sharp teeth.

The neck was taut and its shoulders were hunched on a lean torso, bony knobs running down its spine to the base of its serpentine tail.

At the end of each front arm was a two-claw appendage.

The hind legs were slightly bent at the knees, but then the limbs formed into hocks and withers like a dog; each foot having three bird-like talons.

The chupacabra looked especially creepy in the green imaging.

Jack watched the creature sniffing the air, drawn by the scent of the blood as it moved stealthily toward the bogus goat hidden behind the shrub. He waited until the thing was close enough and stepped out from the concealment.

The chupacabra spotted Jack and turned to bolt.

Jack fired the shotgun.

The rubber bullet struck the creature in the shoulder.

It stumbled forwards, but stayed on its feet.

Jack ratcheted another dum dum into the chamber and shot it again, hitting it squarely in the middle of the back. This time it fell to the ground, kicking its feet and screeched like a cat that had just had its tail pinched under a rocking chair.

Miguel rushed up and shoved the tip of the stun gun into its chest and gave it a sharp jolt of electricity.

The chupacabra jerked convulsively for a few seconds then went rigid.

"Jesus, Miguel."

"Don't worry. I set it for half charge."

Jack leaned over the ugly creature to confirm it was alive and was relieved to see it was still breathing. He picked up the media player, turned it off, and slipped the device into a side pocket of his cargo pants.

Miguel rolled out a thick canvas bag on the ground that resembled a body bag and had air holes in the fabric. He pulled down the long zipper.

Jack and Miguel picked up the chupacabra and slipped it inside the bag. Miguel closed up the zipper and fastened a small padlock so it couldn't be unzipped.

Jack spoke into his two-way radio and told the pilot they were ready to be picked up.

They took off their night vision goggles and gazed up at the stars.

"Beautiful, eh? Kind of reminds me of—" Jack paused when he heard something in the bush behind him. He tucked the butt of the shotgun into his shoulder and aimed at the source of the noise, which sounded like a frantic pack of Pekinese shredding apart a newspaper.

Miguel switched on his flashlight and shined the beam behind the bush.

Four hunched chupacabras shrank away from the light and vanished into the night.

The only pieces left of the piñata were the head, a single leg, and a few tattered strips of paper and cardboard. The hungry bloodsuckers had eaten every scrap of paper mache that had been covered with blood.

Miguel looked at Jack and laughed.

"What's so funny?"

"Sneaky bastards went and ate the candy."

# 2

## DREAM PROJECT

Lucas Finder was the lone occupant on the elevator headed up to Carter Wilde's office. He'd brought his attaché case along, knowing his boss was anxious for an updated progress report. Construction was near completion thank God, but there was still much that needed to be done before the theme park would be ready for Opening Day.

Lucas had been project manager for Wilde Enterprises for the past ten years and had completed many engineering feats around the world. He'd always beaten his deadlines and completed each project under budget, and was graciously compensated for his exemplary achievements, spurring him to take on even more challenging assignments.

But this venture had been unlike building a pharmaceutical manufacturing facility in South Korea or erecting an elegant high-rise hotel in a wealthy Middle Eastern country and embossing WILDE ENTERPRISES over the front entrances.

This had been a seemingly impossible whim of a 62-year-old eccentric multi-billionaire who happened to be the fifth richest man on the planet and had the resources at his fingertips to make a childhood fantasy come true.

Lucas couldn't remember the last time he had gotten more than three hours sleep in one night since starting the $4 billion project, which had been expected to take three years to complete.

His cell phone was constantly ringing, problems occurring on a daily basis, each one a potential setback threatening to push out the scheduled completion date, which was now only weeks away.

There had been times he was so frustrated he'd even contemplated giving his notice then quickly came to his senses when he realized how much he would miss his job and the sacrifices he would have to make. But most of all, it would be admitting failure and disappointing his boss.

The elevator came to an abrupt stop and the doors slid open.

Lucas stepped out onto the top floor of Wilde Enterprises corporate office—Carter Wilde's penthouse office suite.

The mosaic marble floor had recently been buffed and shimmered like the surface of a sparkling lake under a moonlit sky.

An attractive brunette in her mid forties was sitting at a cherry wood custom reception station that looked like a fortress caponier with its parapet of translucent acrylic window risers. She looked up and smiled. "Good morning, Mr. Finder."

"Morning, Katherine."

Katherine Donahue was Carter Wilde's trusted secretary, and had been since Lucas first began traveling up to the 100th floor to visit the eccentric tycoon.

"Would you like for me to order you up something?" Katherine asked.

"I don't think I could eat though coffee would be nice."

"I'll tell them to bring up a pot of Death Wish."

"You're the best," Lucas said. He needed a quick pick-me-up and knew the popular brand would do the trick, having 200% more caffeine than any other coffee drink.

"Go right in. He's expecting you," Katherine said.

"Thank you," Lucas said. He turned and walked past the large pane windows facing out over the cityscape.

Two burly security guards wearing suits stood outside the tall mahogany double doors to Wilde's office. They scrutinized Lucas and for a second he thought they were going to pat him down. Instead one man reached over and dutifully opened a door.

Lucas gave the big man a nod. He walked through the doorway into the office and the door closed briskly behind him.

Carter Wilde was standing behind his desk with his back turned, facing the floor-to-ceiling wall of glass. He made no indication that he heard Lucas enter.

Instead, he jiggled his right arm, and continued to gaze out at the high-rise canopy of spires and rooftops.

Lucas could hear ice *tinkling* in a glass tumbler. It wasn't even ten o'clock in the morning and Carter Wilde was already into the good stuff.

"Why is it, Lucas, when you look down it seems so much farther than when you're on the street looking up?" Wilde said. He turned around to face Lucas.

His goatee was neatly trimmed and his gray hair was slicked back flat against the crown of his skull. He wore a crisp powder-blue shirt, dark blue tie, and a $43,000 Brioni Vanquish II suit.

"Perception?"

"Exactly." Wilde stepped out from behind his desk.

"If you like, I have the latest updates."

"By the look on your face, I'm guessing there are more problems."

It was difficult not to appear glum when he'd been putting out one fire after another trying to keep the project on track. "Yes, there are issues that need to be addressed."

"Give me a sec, Lucas, and we'll go into the War Room." Wilde went over to his well-stocked wet bar to freshen up his drink.

Lucas gazed about the extravagant suite.

One wall was covered with scores of framed photographs of Carter Wilde chumming it up with various top-ranking foreign dignitaries, famous celebrities and movie stars from all around the world, the wealthy elite, and even a couple of presidents.

In the event of a large business gathering, there were upholstered chairs and sofas situated around the room to seat twenty people for a casual meeting.

Lucas looked over at the indoor putting green and noticed the Louis Vuitton designer golf bag was still in the same spot in the corner of the room from the last time he'd been in Wilde's office. Inside the canvas bag was a 14-piece set of gold and platinum Honma golf clubs, which cost more than Lucas' Lexus.

Wilde stepped away from the wet bar and carried his glass across the room. He jabbed a code on a push pad on the wall and a pocket door opened revealing a large conference room—Carter Wilde's War Room.

Lucas followed his boss into the rectangular room, which had once been used for board meetings, but was now exclusively reserved for the project. Only top managers and department heads currently involved in the project were allowed access and all were contractually bound not to discuss any aspects of what went on within these walls, as Wilde was adamant about keeping his pet project as much a secret as possible.

Wilde switched on the recessed lighting.

A blank drop-down 90-inch flat screen hung from the ceiling in the front of the room.

The earth tone painted walls were covered with conceptual artwork, a detailed timeline outlining the scheduled due dates for each stage of development, along with building blueprints and engineering schematics.

Twelve black leather chairs were set up around one end of the 24-foot long solid walnut table. A row of binders was between two bookends in the center, each report identified by department and giving specific breakdowns of activities performed.

Lucas stepped to the other end of the table and joined Wilde, studying the three displays on the table.

The first miniature model looked like a giant blue beetle and was as long as the width of the conference table. It was the mockup of the theme park with the dome closed.

Lucas' design and engineering teams insisted the curvature of the solar panel roof would gather the most sun power, as the theme park had to be self-sustained due to its remote location.

Wilde placed his glass on a cork coaster on the table and stared down at the next model, which was the same size as the first one without the roof.

Lucas watched his boss and knew he was envisioning what the real theme park would look like.

The interior layout comprised of six tiny round plastic buildings and four circular habitats, quality crafted in exquisite detail and arranged inside an oval-shaped diorama on green matting. Each piece was labeled on the top for easy identification.

Lucas did his own visual walkthrough and started at the main entrance imagining he was a guest entering the theme park. Two rows of statues, in the images of the attractions the visitors would be seeing during their stay, flanked a broad pathway that led to the luxurious hotel.

The zookeepers' workstations and sleeping quarters were in a building left of the hotel. Another circular building was to the right of the hotel; this one reserved for security where the surveillance cameras around the park were to be monitored and the armory was kept under lock and key.

Behind the hotel was an enormous round swimming pool.

To its left, the 900,000-gallon aquarium called the Tank.

On the other side of the circular hotel was the Aviary with aerial space reaching up to the height of the dome's ceiling and was flush in places to glass-enclosed balconies providing safe viewing for the guests.

The Bioengineering Laboratory and Animatronics Workshop Complex was centered in the middle of the diorama.

Four other exhibits were in a horseshoe shape and occupied the other half of the grounds: Sea Monster Cove, The Reptile House, Mammoth Arena, and Biped Habitat.

Lucas looked at the third model, which showed the underground network of tunnels that would be used by the zookeepers, maintenance employees, security guards, or anyone else that needed to travel about the park, preferably unseen by the guests.

Wilde was insistent all operations be seamless to the general public, especially the livestock that would eventually be kept below ground in pens situated around the park as food for the attractions. No parent wanted his or her child witnessing the brutal slaying of a defenseless animal.

The model also showed the intricate maze of electrical conduits, the sewage system, plumbing, and the utility grids for generating solar electricity.

Lucas put his attaché case on the table. He released the catches, and opened the lid. He took out a folder, the latest progress report.

Wilde picked up his drink. He took a sip and kept staring at the second model. "Okay, Lucas. Let's hear it."

Lucas began going down his checklist. "There's been a repeated malfunction with one of the elevators in the hotel."

"Go on," Wilde said. He turned to face Lucas and sat on the edge of the table.

"Our maintenance manager has voiced concern about the Tank."

"What kind of concern?" Wilde asked.

"About an apparent problem with the filtration system in the aquarium."

"Does he know the cause?"

"Not at this time."

"What else?"

"Park Security has been complaining about computer glitches affecting the surveillance cameras. I sent out our best I.T. person."

"Any more breakthroughs at the lab?"

"Yes, both Dr. McCabe and Professor Howard have made incredible progress. I think you will be very pleased. You'll love what the Workshop has come up with."

"I look forward to it. So, if we remedy these problems, when do you think everything will be done?"

"We won't be able to have a firm date until after the inspections."

"I thought everything was signed off?"

"Well, there's been a bit of a disruption."

"What's the holdup?"

"Federal regulatory authorities. I'm afraid there's been a leak. The USDA and the Department of Health and Human Services is concerned we're violating the Animal Welfare Act."

Wilde slammed his glass down, spilling his malt scotch on the table. "How can they say that when we're bioengineering and cloning creatures that haven't even existed until now?"

"That's why they're stalling. I'd hate to see it get to the Supreme Court."

"I'll make sure that never happens," Wilde said.

"The last thing you want is a bunch of angry animal activists picketing the main gate on Opening Day," Lucas said, knowing how his boss hated negative publicity.

"Then I think it's time we send in the marketing and advertising teams," Wilde said. "Let them experience the park for themselves. Create such a buzz no one's going to care about those ranting sign-waving lunatics."

"Don't you think we should correct the existing problems first?"

"Nonsense," Wilde said. "Now is the time to prepare our ad campaign."

"Shouldn't our first priority be public safety?"

"Lucas, don't you think every person knows there's a certain amount of risk every time they go to an amusement park?"

"Honestly, no. We just assume everything will be fine."

"Get the ball rolling."

"Yes, sir," Lucas said. He dropped the progress report inside his attaché case and closed it in preparation to leave.

"I want this to be a family experience," Wilde said, ushering Lucas out of the War Room.

"I'll draft an email."

"Tell them to be packed and ready for a redeye tonight."

Lucas turned and looked at his boss. "Sir, don't you think that's a little short notice. I mean—"

"Have Katherine arrange to have the company's 737 fueled and waiting at the Jet Center," Wilde said, turning his attention to the view outside and ending their meeting.

# 3

## CHANGE OF PLANS

Nick Wells pulled up in his driveway. He glanced at the clock on the dash, surprised to see it was only two in the afternoon. Normally, Meg would be ecstatic having him home from work so early. Maybe even squeeze some time in between the sheets before Gabe came home from school but he doubted that was going to happen.

He shut off the engine and sat behind the steering wheel for a moment wondering how he was going to drop the bombshell on his wife. Before leaving work, he had called the hotel where he had booked a suite to celebrate their anniversary and cancelled the reservation. He'd also called his mother and told her Gabe wouldn't be staying the weekend with her after all and that he was sorry, as he knew how much she was looking forward to spending some time with her grandson.

He grabbed his workbag off the passenger seat and got out of the car.

Walking up to the front door he noticed the lawn needed mowing.

Lately, Gabe had been neglecting his chores. Meg had been on Nick's case, saying he was too lenient with their fourteen-year-old son and needed to be more assertive.

Nick had been swamped bringing his work home most evenings and usually only saw his son at dinner before the boy went out to spend time with his friends.

He remembered his father being a heavy-handed disciplinarian, something that Nick promised he wouldn't be raising his own child. The last thing he wanted was to browbeat his son and strain their relationship, especially when he rarely saw him.

Nick unlocked the front door and went inside. "I'm home!"

"In here," Meg called out.

Nick walked through the living room. He took off his coat and draped it over the back of the sofa and tossed his workbag on a cushion.

He came into the kitchen, loosened his tie, and went straight for the refrigerator.

Meg was standing at the counter, preparing a roast for dinner. "You're home early." She gave him a concerned look. "Please, don't tell me you're sick."

"No, no. I'm fine," Nick said. He opened the fridge door and took out a bottle of Michelob Ultra Light. He unscrewed the cap, opened the cabinet door under the sink, and tossed the cap into the trash bin.

He leaned against the countertop and watched Meg put the roasting pan in the oven. "There's been a slight change in our plans."

"What do you mean?" Meg said. "Don't tell me they're making you work."

"You got it."

"Damn it, Nick. This is our weekend!"

"Honey, let me explain. I'm going on a business trip and you and Gabe are coming along."

"Where?"

"Well, that's the thing. I'm really not sure."

"You have no idea where we're going? Seriously, Nick? And what are we supposed to do? Sit around the hotel while you work? So why is this business trip so important?"

"It's some secret project the company's been working on. They want us to go out and do an assessment."

"What, write a bunch of bogus reviews on Yelp?"

"Very funny."

"I need a drink." Meg opened a cabinet door. She took down a bottle of Merlot and grabbed a water glass from the drying rack. She filled the glass almost to the rim with red wine, and took a long sip. "So what is this secret project the company's been working on? And please don't say, if you tell me you're going to have to kill me."

"All I know is that it's a theme park."

"We're spending our fifteenth wedding anniversary at Knott's Berry Farm?"

"Did I mention we would be staying at a luxurious five-star hotel?"

"Now you're talking," Meg said and drank some more wine.

"With an Olympic-size pool."

"Even better. Gabe will like that."

"You'll be glad to know that Bob and Rhonda will be going, so you gals can hang out."

"Does that mean Shane, too?"

"I'm sure they'll be bringing him along. Why, what's wrong?"

"Ever since Gabe started going over to their house, he's been acting strangely. Did I tell you he slammed the door on me when I told him to clean up his room?"

"When was this?" Nick asked.

"This morning, after you left. I also smelled pot in his room."

"Pot?"

"I think he gets it from Shane. I'm telling you, the boy's a bad influence."

"I'll talk to Bob."

"You better talk to Gabe as well."

"I will." Nick drank the rest of his beer and put the empty bottle on the countertop. He reached inside the fridge and grabbed another beer.

"So when are we leaving?" Meg asked.

Nick hesitated for a moment before answering. "A company driver will be picking us up tonight around eleven."

"What?" Meg almost spilled her wine. "Jesus, Nick."

"How long till dinner?"

"The roast should be done in an hour."

"That'll give us a little time to do some packing."

Meg rushed out of the kitchen and headed down the hallway.

Nick followed her into the bedroom. He opened the sliding closet door and took out two travel bags on wheels. He laid the luggage on the bed, unzipped each one, and opened them up.

He sat on the edge of the bed and watched Meg going through the dresser drawers on her side of the bureau. "You know, there's a chance we might have to share a room with Gabe."

Meg stopped and looked at Nick.

She was holding a white two-piece bathing suit. Nick's favorite.

Meg tossed the swimsuit into her suitcase. "That roast better not burn."

"Then I suggest we get cooking," Nick said, tearing off his shirt.

# 4

## MYSTERY FLIGHT

The company driver had been prompt, picking Nick and his family up from their house. They arrived just before midnight at the part of the airport reserved for private jets.

Nick saw a long line of people ready to go up the stairs to board a 737 airliner with WILDE ENTERPRISES blazed across the side of the fuselage and the tail section.

Baggage handlers were collecting everyone's suitcases, making sure there were tags with the owners' names on each piece of luggage, loading them on carts to take over and stow in the cargo hold.

Nick recognized only a few employees from his department, figuring that many of them worked on separate floors in the corporate building.

It was first-come, first-served so everyone could sit wherever they wanted.

They were shuffling down the aisle when Nick spotted Bob Pascale standing behind a seatback a few rows back. "Hey, Nick! We saved you some seats."

The two families shared greetings and everyone grabbed a seat.

Gabe and Shane sat together in one row with Bob on the aisle seat. Nick sat in the seat across the aisle from Bob. Meg sat in the middle seat beside Nick and Rhonda was by the window.

Nick noticed all of the sun visors were pulled down covering the windows, which was probably standard operational procedure for a redeye so passengers could grab some sleep during the flight.

He glanced over at Meg. "How's your head?"

"Remind me to stay away from red wine," she replied. She delved in her purse and took out a bottle of Tylenol. She washed down three pills with water she'd brought along.

"This sucks," Rhonda said.

Nick leaned forward. "What's wrong?"

"I can't open the stupid visor."

"Maybe it's stuck."

Rhonda tried again but it wouldn't budge. "See what I'm saying."

"There's some open seats by the windows if you want to switch."

"No, that's okay. I'll probably get some sleep."

Nick knew everyone was onboard and seated because the forward exit door was closing. Outside, the powerful turbine engines began to rev, vibrating the passenger compartment.

A flight attendant stood in the front aisle and grabbed a mike from a holder mounted on the bulkhead. "Good morning everyone and welcome aboard. Before we take off, Mr. Wilde has asked everyone to surrender their cell phones, laptops, iPads, cameras, and any other electronic device you might have on your person. A flight attendant will be coming down the aisle to pick them up. Please, don't be alarmed. All your belongings will be returned to you on your return flight."

Nick could hear people grumbling.

One person spoke up. "This is absurd. How are we supposed to do our jobs without our computers?"

"Mr. Wilde was quite adamant that you surrender all devices."

"Ain't this some weird shit," Bob said, looking over at Nick.

"He's the boss," Nick replied.

Weird shit was right.

He'd never heard of such a request.

Meg nudged him in the side. "Nick, what's going on? Why do we have to give up our phones?"

"Must be because of the project. Probably afraid someone will take pictures and post them online."

"Couldn't he just ask everyone not to take pictures? I have to say I'm feeling a little violated here. Gabe is going to go nuts without his iPad."

"It'll be good for him to take a break from that thing."

"We're just going to hand over our phones?"

"Rules are rules."

"Okay," Meg said. "Just so you know, I really think this is a bad idea. How do we know someone won't be going through our phones, stealing our personal information?"

"They wouldn't do that."

"Are you sure?"

Nick leaned out and looked back. A flight attendant was pushing a cart down the aisle, stopping at each row, collecting passengers' electronic devices.

He took his cell phone out of his trouser pocket and made sure it was turned off to save the battery.

Rhonda and Meg gave their phones to Nick.

He looked over and saw that Bob had collected the devices from the boys and they weren't happy. Bob glanced at Nick and shook his head with a bewildered expression.

When the flight attendant stopped at their row, she asked their names and whose device was which. Her tone was businesslike and wasn't at all friendly. Nick handed her the phones. She applied an identifying sticker to each one so it could be returned to the rightful owner and dropped them in an already half filled plastic bin.

Once she was done, she shoved the cart up to the next row.

Nick had a queasy feeling in his gut.

Like a captured soldier who'd just handed over his gun to the enemy.

# 5

## TAKEN FOR A RIDE

Nick figured they'd been in the air just over three hours when the plane finally made its descent and came in for a landing. During the earlier part of the flight he'd heard whispering voices, more passengers protesting about having to give up their phones, but after a while everyone began to settle down, either resigning to the fact that they had no choice in the matter as it had been a directive from the higher echelon or were too tired to complain due to the lateness of the hour.

The commercial jet came to a complete stop and the engines shut down.

On a normal flight, passengers would be getting up from their seats, scrambling to get their carry-ons out from the overheads, but in this case there were no belongings to retrieve.

Instead, everyone remained seated like an obedient classroom of children awaiting the teacher's permission to stand.

Minutes passed, but neither of the flight attendants made an effort to open the exit door or speak on the public address system to explain what was happening next.

Bob leaned out in the aisle and said to Nick, "They're stalling while they offload our luggage."

"But why?"

"No doubt going through our bags looking for computers or cameras."

"I have to say, this is getting to be one crazy trip."

"I'll say," Bob said.

Nick sat forward so he could see Gabe. "How's it going son?"

"I can't believe you let them take my iPad," Gabe said, straining against his seatbelt and glaring at his father.

"Sorry, but it's company policy."

"Company bullshit you mean," Gabe snarled.

"Watch it!"

Gabe slammed back in his seat.

"Did he just say *bullshit*?" Meg asked, gripping Nick's forearm.

"Kid must be having Wi-Fi withdrawals."

"This isn't funny, Nick. I'm getting worried."

"Everything will be fine. Once we get off this damn plane."

"I wish I could see outside," Rhonda said.

"Yeah, sure would be nice to know where we are," Meg told her friend.

"Wait a minute, I think they're going to announce something," Nick said when he saw one of the flight attendants up front with the mike in her hand.

"I hope you all enjoyed your flight. When you disembark there will be someone that will direct you to your bus. Thank you for flying Wilde Enterprises."

"Thank God," Bob said, grabbing the headrest of the seat in front of him and pulling himself up to stand.

The passengers nearest the aisle got up and formed a single line. People in the middle seats crouched under the overheads, while those by the windows remained seated, waiting their turns.

A flight attendant opened the exit door. She smiled at each passenger as they disembarked.

Nick and his family were the last to leave. He couldn't help noticing the way the flight attendant looked at him, all smug and superior. He wanted nothing better than to wipe the condescending smile off her face. It irked him knowing they worked for the same company and neither of them had any real authority over the other, yet here he was, kowtowing to another peer.

Outside, as he came down the stairs, he was shocked to see that they had landed on a remote airstrip and not at a commercial airport.

"Where are we?" Meg asked, stepping onto the tarmac.

"I have no idea," Nick said. He looked around and saw runway lights stretching into the darkness. A generator was running, supplying power to a few extremely bright portable spotlights that made it impossible to see the surrounding terrain, which might have given a hint where they were.

A Wilde Enterprises employee with a clipboard was assisting passengers and pointing them in the direction of two black charter buses parked nearby.

After being assigned their bus, Nick and his family went over and began to board.

Meg and Gabe got on first. Nick could hear the bus driver greet them. He grabbed the hand railing and stepped up into the bus. The bus driver sat sideways in his chair and gave Nick a friendly smile. "Welcome aboard."

Nick responded with a grunt. He felt drained from the flight and was in dire need of some sleep.

"Rough flight?"

"You might say that," Nick replied not wanting to appear rude. At least this guy was making an attempt to be decent, unlike those harpy flight attendants. He glanced at the nametag on the driver's shirt: Sam Kerry.

"So Sam, how long till we're there?"

"Time enough to squeeze in a power nap."

"I could use one."

"Go grab a seat. We're about to pull out." Sam grabbed a lever and the side door hissed closed.

Nick made his way down the aisle.

He counted maybe forty people on board, some of them already taking the opportunity to grab some much-needed sleep as the interior lights were dimmed.

He saw Bob and Rhonda already seated.

"Watch, after this, we'll be on some damn camel ride across the desert," Bob said.

"I wouldn't joke," Nick said. "Where's Shane?"

"He went back with Gabe."

"Might as well grab some shuteye."

"Yeah, it's been a long night," Bob said, nodding his head at Rhonda who was already fast asleep.

"You mean morning."

"Yeah. Sweet dreams, Nick," Bob said and closed his eyes.

Nick continued to the back of the bus. Meg had moved over to the window seat and Nick sat down beside her. "How does your head feel now?"

"Like I have jet lag."

"So much for a fun start to our impromptu vacation." Nick glanced across the aisle. His son had bundled his jacket into a pillow and was sleeping with his head rested against the window.

Shane had raised the center armrest and was curled up on two seats in the row behind Gabe and was fast asleep.

"I hope he isn't going to sulk the whole weekend," Meg said.

"I'm sure there'll be plenty to do to get Gabe's mind off of his iPad. At least, there better be or he's going to be unbearable to be around." He turned to Meg. She had her hands cupped over the window and was trying to look out.

"What do you see?"

"Nothing."

"Maybe when we get on the road—"

"No, Nick. I can't see anything. This isn't tinted glass, it's a plastic panel."

"Are you sure?" Nick leaned over and tried peering out. She was right. All he could see was their faces reflected off the dark surface.

The diesel engine started up with a rumble.

Nick looked up front. He was relieved to see the glow of the outside spotlights through the windshield. If anything, he could gaze out the windshield and see where they were going.

A motorized black screen began to drop down behind the bus driver's seat. The divider was the width of the bus's interior and reached down to the floor, blocking the passengers' view of the windshield.

"What the hell?"

"What's wrong?" Meg asked.

"A panel just came down behind the driver so we can't see out." Nick was tempted to run up the aisle and demand the screen be raised, but then the bus pulled out of the parking lot and was making a slow wide turn.

"Nick, this doesn't feel right. First they take away our phones, now we're being transported to who knows where."

When Meg used the word *transported* he couldn't help thinking of those big rigs he'd see on the freeway, the ones hauling livestock to the slaughterhouse.

And then another unsettling thought came to mind when he considered their current situation—prisoners in railcars being taken to the death camps.

# 6

## FIRST IMPRESSION

Nick wasn't sure how long he'd been asleep when the bus came to a stop and he woke up. He looked over at Meg and gave her a nudge. "I think we're here."

"Huh?" Meg yawned and stretched her arms over her head.

The overhead lights brightened the cabin and the divider behind the bus driver rose.

Nick glanced over at Gabe. His son was awake. He'd unraveled his coat and was putting it on. Shane was sitting up, rubbing his eyes.

"This is it," Nick said.

"When do we eat, I'm starving," was Gabe's reply.

"Yeah, they better have some decent food," Shane whined.

"I'm sure they will," Nick said. He heard a blast of air and knew the front door had opened, which was everyone's cue to get up from their seats. "You boys go ahead, we'll be right behind you," he said to Gabe.

The teenagers stepped into the aisle and got in line behind the others.

When Nick stood, he caught a glimpse of the outdoors through the windshield. It was twilight and he could see ragged silhouettes.

Nick stepped back and let Meg go in front of him. They were the last ones in line so he put his arms around her waist and gave her a kiss on the cheek. "Ready for our big adventure?"

She looked back at him. "What I really want is a shower."

They shuffled forward to the front of the bus.

Sam Kerry was standing outside, assisting anyone that needed help coming down off the steps.

"You folks have a wonderful day," Sam said as Nick stepped out of the bus. Nick saw men wearing matching polo shirts and trousers, offloading bags from both the storage compartments on the buses and taking them over to flatbed trailers hooked to the back of two separate golf carts.

"What happens now?" Nick asked.

"Now you walk. Don't worry, it's not far."

Nick stepped out from between the two buses, surprised to see they were smack dab in the middle of nowhere in a giant forest of 100-foot pines and red firs.

Meg stared at the trees. "Nick, please don't tell me this is going to be one of those survivalist weekends?"

"No one mentioned peer bonding to me." Nick turned to Bob who was standing next to him.

"At this point," Bob said, "nothing would surprise me."

A round helicopter-landing pad with the Wilde Enterprises logo was not too far from where the buses were parked.

Once the baggage was loaded, the workers jumped on the back of the golf carts and the drivers headed up a paved road into the trees.

A carved wooden sign with the words ENTRANCE was at the trailhead of a groomed pathway bordered with split-rail fencing. The walkway ran parallel with the road and was separated by a thin stand of trees.

Everyone assumed that was the way and started up the path.

Nick and Bob's families were at the end of the procession.

"I hear something coming." Rhonda stopped to listen.

"Sounds like a truck," Nick said.

"Better be a taco truck," Shane said. He jabbed Gabe and they both started laughing.

Nick caught a glimpse of the big rig between the trees as the vehicle drove by.

"Anyone get a good look?" Meg asked.

"I did," Bob replied. "Looked like a cattle truck. That road must lead to a main highway."

Nick noticed that everyone in front of them had come to a stop and were staring up. He couldn't tell exactly at what, as the treetops were blocking his view.

As he approached, he could hear people murmuring, some even gasping.

A woman hysterically blurted out, "Oh my God, it's an alien spaceship!"

"It's a giant beetle," a little boy shouted.

Nick gazed up and couldn't believe what he was seeing.

"Jesus, they built a football stadium in the middle of the forest?" Bob said.

"This is amazing," Nick said. He had to agree with the boy's first reaction, the structure did look like a turquoise beetle. The sloping roof had to be a least 250 feet tall at its highest point, which was near the center, and had to encompass an area close to 100 acres. It appeared to be made up of flat solar panels, which made perfect sense, as there was no telling how far away the nearest power station was located.

Nick heard a woman call out, "Over here, folks!"

Four employees wearing similar polo shirts and pants were standing just outside the main entrance of the dome stadium. Two more men in black shirts were posted as sentries. When one of them turned, Nick saw SECURITY stenciled on the back of his shirt.

Everyone mustered in a half circle.

"Good morning. My name is Christine Olson and we will be your tour guides throughout your stay with us. We will be breaking up into four groups. When one of us calls your name, please assemble in front of your designated tour guide. This should only take a few minutes."

Nick watched as families peeled off and congregated in small groups when their names were called. When Christine called out Nick's name she waved for him and his family to join her group. He was glad to see that Bob, Rhonda, and Shane were also included along with fourteen other people.

Once everyone had been assigned a group, Christine led the way through the front entrance.

It was like entering a gargantuan cavern, but instead of a rock floor and stalagmites, the grounds were teeming with trees and meticulous landscaping.

The steel girded ceiling loomed 250 feet above their heads like the underside of a giant umbrella.

Nick looked up at the mammoth wrought iron archway:

**WELCOME TO CRYPTID ZOO**

Meg scowled at Nick and whispered, "Really, Nick? They put us through all this for a stupid zoo?"

Nick shrugged as they walked under the span and continued down the wide flagstone path bordered on each side by what appeared to be columns of statues that stood twenty feet tall and were covered with large tarps. He saw a bare pedestal the size of an above ground hot tub, with the word *MNGWA* on a bronze plaque, which made no sense.

They came to a junction with signs where the walkway forked. To the left was a two-story round building designated for the ZOOKEEPERS & PARK STAFF. An identical looking building was to the right and was SECURITY.

Nick expected their tour guide to make mention of the two buildings, but she didn't, and they kept walking straight toward the circular five-story glass-front hotel.

When they reached the front steps, Christine stopped and turned around. "When we go inside, would the employees in our group please follow me to the registration desk and we will get your key cards. You should be glad to know that your bags have already been brought up to your rooms. I imagine many of you are exhausted and would like some time to rest and freshen up so we have scheduled a late lunch and our first two tours for this afternoon. Please, follow me."

Nick and Meg had been to Las Vegas a few times and had stayed on the strip where the hotels had outlandish themes like the castle at Excalibur and the pirate ship show at Treasure Island.

Being that this was a zoo, he was expecting an animal theme of some sort when he stepped into the lobby. He was pleasantly surprised to find the large antechamber tastefully decorated. The marble flooring gleamed under the spiral design of recessed lights. Black leather chairs and couches were positioned about the reception area offering an intimate setting for a rendezvous and a place for guests to gather. The vestibule was adorned with magnificent twelve-foot tall palm trees in giant pots.

Nick and Bob, along with a man and woman that Nick had never met, followed Christine up to the front desk. She told the hotel clerk their names and was handed the key cards.

Once she had given everyone their magnetic room keys, Christine said, "You will find packets in your rooms that will outline Mr. Wilde's expectations and the guidelines you will be following evaluating the theme park. But we'll talk more about that later. Now I suggest everyone get some proper sleep. Oh, and for those of you that are hungry, you'll find baskets of assorted fruit and pastries as well as tea, coffee, and juice waiting for you in your rooms."

She glanced at her wristwatch. "It's a little before seven right now. Let's all meet here in the lobby at one o'clock sharp. Any questions?"

"Ah, yeah," Nick said, but then he looked around and saw the tired faces. "It can wait."

"Great," Christine said. "See you all then."

# 7

## SECOND THOUGHTS

Jack drove the cargo van down the service road and stopped at the dropdown barrier bar blocking the side entrance to the massive dome. He rolled his window down when the security guard stepped out of the booth and approached the vehicle.

"Morning, Ralph," Jack said, raising his ID badge on the end of the lanyard hanging around his neck for the man to inspect.

"Mr. Tremens, nice to see you," the guard said. He glanced inside the cab at Miguel sitting in the passenger seat. Miguel displayed his badge.

"Mr. Walla."

Something shrieked and banged around in the back of the van.

The guard tried to see into the cargo hold, but a curtain blocked his view. He looked at Jack. "Live one, eh?"

"Yeah, and it's not too happy," Jack said.

"You're clear to go."

"Thanks." Jack waited for the bar to rise then drove through and down a ramp into a large tunnel. He followed the brightly lit underground passage for a short distance to an intersection and turned left to where it opened up to a small parking area.

He made a U-turn and backed the van into a stall a few feet short of a wall with a door.

Jack turned off the engine and jumped out. He walked around to the rear of the van. Miguel was already opening the rear doors.

As soon as the chupacabra saw the two men, it reached out through the bars of its cage and hissed at them, jerking its head side to side like a twitchy drug addict. The creature screeched, pulled its arm back in between the bars, and rattled its cage.

"Calm down, no one is going to hurt you," Jack said.

Miguel grabbed the stun gun pole and showed it to the chupacabra. Its eyes widened with fear and it slunk back in its cage. Miguel stared at the creature. "You remembered."

"So it has long term memory," Jack said. "We'll have to pass that along." He went over and retrieved a flatbed pushcart that had been left parked beside the wall. He shoved the edge of the cart just under the rear bumper.

"Better be careful. It loves to bite," Miguel said.

"Yeah, you're right." Jack took a moment to put on a thick pair of gloves. He waited until Miguel had his on before they pulled the cage out of the van and loaded it onto the cart.

Miguel kept the stun gun pole and closed the rear doors of the van. He hurried over and opened the door for Jack so he could push the cart inside. They followed the dimly lit corridor until they reached an elevator.

They took the elevator from the sub-basement up to the first floor.

The elevator doors parted and Jack pushed the cart out into a hallway with bright overhead fluorescent bulbs. The chupacabra being a nocturnal creature immediately reacted to the blinding light. It cowered in a corner of the cage and let out an ear-piercing squeal.

Jack took his coat off and draped the garment over the cage to block the glare. He stood behind the pushcart, but didn't move.

He listened to the creature whimpering, huddled under the protective shade.

"What is it, Jack?" Miguel asked.

"I don't know. I'm kind of feeling sorry for it."

"That ugly thing? Don't tell me you're turning into a softie?"

"I'm starting to have reservations if what we're doing is really right."

"It's no different than any other job we've taken on."

"Yeah, well, capturing endangered animals so they can be protected is one thing. This feels more like we're creating a freak show."

"Maybe we are," Miguel said. "But that's what people want to see."

"And that makes it right?"

"I don't know what to tell you. Maybe you should talk it over with Professor Howard and explain how you feel."

"I doubt she'll understand. Not with all the breakthroughs she's been having."

"You have to admit, they are astonishing," Miguel said.

"We better get to the lab," Jack said and began pushing the cart down the hall.

They came to a bank of windows and could see inside a large laboratory.

A woman with frizzy blonde hair was sitting at a table, peering into the eyepiece of a high-powered microscope. When she looked up, she saw Jack through the glass and gave him a friendly wave. She got up and crossed the room. She was wearing a white lab coat, skirt, and flat shoes.

Jack thought Nora looked anemic and knew she'd been running herself ragged working long hours, forsaking her health for her research. He heard a buzz and the door to the lab opened.

"Hello, Jack," Nora said.

"We brought you a surprise." Jack pushed the cart through the doorway.

Miguel followed and the door swished closed behind him. "Morning, Professor Howard."

"Morning, Miguel. So what is it?"

Jack went down on one knee and beckoned for Nora to join him. "Take a peek, but don't get too close."

Nora crouched and looked inside the cage. "Oh my God, Jack. You were able to capture one alive?"

"Finally, yeah." Until now, Jack and Miguel had been unsuccessful in the past trying to capture a chupacabra and had only been able to bring the scientist a dead specimen they'd found in the desert.

"This is incredible," Nora said.

"What's incredible?" a man's voice said from across the room.

Jack stood and saw Dr. Joel McCabe walking toward them. His beard was bushy as always and his lab coat had a few smudges of blood on the front.

"We got lucky," Jack said. "Trapped you a real one."

"That right." Dr. McCabe directed Jack's attention to a large window with thick laminated tempered glass facing into a small enclosure.

Jack could see four chupacabras, stooped over, and cowering on the floor with their hands over their heads. They looked identical in every way, somewhat like the creature in the cage. He was surprised to see the bioengineer had been able to replicate the cryptids in such a short span of time from the DNA extracted from the dead chupacabra that Jack and Miguel had supplied.

"Seems you boys needn't have bothered." Dr. McCabe crossed his arms and grinned.

"There's still a lot you can learn from this one," Jack said, always finding the man to be irritating and self-righteous.

"Like what?"

"That chupacabras are nocturnal."

"I know that."

"Then turn down the lights. It's too bright in there, you're scaring them. That's why this cage is covered," Jack said.

Nora lifted part of Jack's coat to get a better look at the chupacabra. "Oh my God, I just realized."

"What is it?" Jack asked.

"You guys found a female and she's pregnant."

"Really?"

"Do you realize what this means? I might actually be able to perform a somatic cell nuclear transfer."

"You mean...?"

"This is another creature we can clone. Isn't that wonderful?" Nora was so excited she jumped to her feet and began to swoon.

Jack caught her before she fell. "Nora, are you okay?"

"I just got a little dizzy there for a second."

"When's the last time you ate?"

Nora gave him a blank expression.

"Let's go get you something to eat. This can wait."

Miguel looked around the lab. He grabbed a lab coat off a hook on the wall. He slowly removed Jack's coat, replacing it with the smock, and covered the top of the cage.

"Thanks," Jack said, putting on his jacket. He glanced over at McCabe while Nora was taking off her lab coat. Jack could tell McCabe wasn't too thrilled he was whisking Nora away and was probably the reason she'd been driving herself so hard trying to stay out of the way of the arrogant prick.

Nora tucked her blouse in the waistband of her skirt and took a moment to brush out her hair. "I'm ready."

Miguel held the door for Nora and Jack and followed them out into the hall.

McCabe watched them leave through the window.

Once they were gone, he went over to a workbench and opened a drawer. He took out a flashlight and put it inside the pocket of his lab coat.

Then he opened a medicine cabinet.

He filled the plunger on a hypodermic needle with a liquid sedative.

McCabe leaned down and peered at the creature hunkered inside the cage.

The chupacabra glared at him and hissed, like a snake about to strike.

McCabe ripped the lab coat off the cage and shined the flashlight directly into the chupacabra's face.

The creature squealed and slammed against the bars.

"Lights out," McCabe said and jabbed the needle into its arm.

The chupacabra buckled and collapsed on the floor of the cage.

# 8

## THE TANK

Meg stood in front of the bathroom mirror wearing only her bra and panties and applied her makeup. Her shoulder length hair was damp after her shower. She finished with her mascara and switched on the blow dryer.

"You better get a move on," Nick called out from the other room, but he doubted if she could hear him. He went over and sat at the desk. He turned on the reading lamp and pulled open the single drawer. Inside were packets filled with questionnaires and evaluation forms with a five-page instruction sheet and a thin 3-ring binder. He took a moment to read through the instructions.

Meg turned off the hairdryer. She went into the suite where she had laid out her clothes on the bed and started to get dressed. "I do love our privacy, but do you really think it was smart letting Gabe and Shane share a room?"

"Bob seemed to think it was okay. Besides, the boys are in an adjacent room. Bob said he could pop in on them when they least expected it to make sure they were staying out of trouble."

"And how often would that be?" Meg said, pulling her T-shirt down over her head.

"I trust Gabe."

"It's Shane I'm worried about."

"It'll be okay."

"If you say so." Meg gave her hair a quick brushing out. "I'm ready if you are."

Nick checked his watch. They had only minutes before they were supposed to be down in the lobby. He made sure he had his key card and brought along the 3-ring binder.

When they came out of the room, Bob, Rhonda, and the boys were waiting by the elevator.

"You guys get enough rest?" Nick asked.

Rhonda nodded with a smile.

Gabe and Shane looked a little blurry-eyed and their hair was uncombed, as they'd probably stayed up fooling around when they should have been getting some sleep.

"You bet," Bob replied. He saw the binder in Nick's hand and raised his own. "Ready to critique the hell out of this place?"

"Let's hope it's a no-brainer and they have a 5-star restaurant," Nick said. "I'm famished."

When they got down to the lobby, Christine was waiting with the rest of the members of her tour group. "Good, we're all here," she said once she saw Nick and the others approaching.

Christine led the way through the lobby to a large dining area with thirty white linen tables, each with enough chairs to sit four to six people. Crystal chandeliers hung from the ceiling. The first thing Nick noticed was the chemical, formaldehyde smell of what looked like newly laid carpet. Definitely points off for that.

Another tour group was filing out a side door. They'd left behind a dozen tables cluttered with dirty dishes. Two busboys were doing their best, busily clearing the tables to get ready for the next batch of diners. They arranged clean plates and cutlery on the last table and carried their full tote bins through the swinging double doors into the kitchen.

Christine smiled at everyone and graciously swept her arm back toward the dining room. "I'll leave you to enjoy our wonderful buffet. I'll be back in forty-five minutes so we can start our first tour."

A few people went over to claim a table while their family members got in line to get their food. A long buffet counter with a glass sneeze guard ran along one side of the dining room. Two employees wearing white paper hats and white jackets were standing behind the serving trays, ready to carve up roast beef or delve out turkey slices.

After Nick filled his plate, he went over and sat with his family. Bob, Rhonda, and Shane came over and joined them at their table. They were so hungry that no one spoke at first as they dove into their meals.

Once Nick and Bob had finished eating, they pushed their plates to the side and opened their binders to get everyone's comments on their meals.

Gabe and Shane had no complaints and had even gone back for seconds. Nick figured their taste buds were so accustomed to fast food they could hardly be expected to be good judges of anything that wasn't fried or stuffed between two buns.

Meg said her omelet tasted like it had been made with powdered eggs.

Rhonda hadn't been so keen on her eggs benedict as she preferred béarnaise to the hollandaise sauce and pointed out that her knife and fork hadn't been thoroughly washed, as there was still crusted food on the silverware.

Bob thought the turkey was dry and had no flavor and the mashed potatoes were lumpy.

Nick's roast beef tasted more like lamb and was a little gamy.

Needless to say, they weren't able to give the restaurant a favorable write-up.

While Meg, Rhonda, and the boys went off to the restroom, Nick and Bob stayed behind to compare notes.

"Is it me, or does this place seemed understaffed?" Bob said.

"Yeah, it does. Like they weren't expecting us."

"And what's with the lousy food. I hope they don't think hotels guests are going to enjoy this. I've eaten better in a cafeteria."

"It was pretty bad."

"Bit of a bust, if you ask me," Bob said, closing his binder.

"I totally agree," Nick said. He spotted Meg and Rhonda coming out of the restroom.

Gabe and Shane were clowning around by the drinking fountain, getting each other wet. Meg and Rhonda shooed them along.

Nick looked across the dining room and saw Christine waving for everyone to come and join her by the side exit. "Let's hope the tour's better than the food."

They filed out slowly onto a poolside area with rows of chaise lounges surrounding a circular Olympic-size gunite swimming pool. The chlorinated water seemed sparkling clear, but it was difficult to be sure with the black bottom.

Nick gazed up and had to shade his eyes from the bright lights high above in the girders, which together seemed like natural sunlight and was probably why the lawns and trees looked so healthy. He became quickly disillusioned when he realized a small patch of lawn nearby was actually artificial turf and there was a plastic leaf on the ground under a fake Japanese plum tree.

Christine led them down a flagstone path toward a windowless building four stories high. Above the entrance door were the words THE TANK in a giant wavy font bordered with stingrays and tropical fish caricatures.

As soon as they entered the building, Nick could feel the temperature drop a few degrees and was rather chilly. He looked over at Meg. She was rubbing her arms to warm them up.

"Should have brought along a sweater," she said.

Nick looked up and saw that the ceiling was thirty feet high.

"Check it out!" Shane said, gazing up at the massive mural that had to be at least thirty feet long and twenty feet high. It was an artist's rendition of a giant squid attacking a sailing frigate on the open seas. The creature's head was visible below the bow of the ship, its tentacles wrapping around booms and scaling masts. Sailors were jumping into the rough surf to escape being killed, others dangling over the decks, held captive and being crushed by the enormous tentacles.

Nick thought the depiction seemed rather violent for a family theme park and made a mental note to put that in his report.

"What is that?" Meg asked, staring at the mural.

"That's a kraken, Mom," Gabe said.

"Wasn't there a kraken in that Sam Worthington movie?"

"That's right. Clash of the Titans."

"I don't remember it looking anything like this."

"This way please," Christine called out.

Everyone followed the tour guide around a bend into an observation area where the lights were dimmed low, accentuating the bluish waters inside a gigantic aquarium.

"Welcome to the Tank," Christine said loud enough for everyone to hear, her voice echoing in the cavernous room. "Please assemble along the hand railing so that you can all see." Once everyone was situated, she continued by saying, "The Tank is 120 feet across, 65 feet deep, and 35 feet high and contains just over 900,000 gallons of salinated water."

Nick had taken Meg and Gabe to the Monterrey Bay Aquarium a couple of years ago and remembered he was rather impressed with all the exhibits. He didn't see anything spectacular here; especially not enough to draw visitors to want to travel all the way out to such a remote location.

Teems of fish were swimming around an 80-foot wide coral reef in the middle of the aquarium: sunfish, dolphins, groupers, rockfish, leopard and sand sharks, stingrays, bluefin tuna, and swarming schools of sardines and shiner surfperch, all disappearing around one end to eventually reappear from the other side.

There were also large predators: an eighteen-foot long great white shark and half a dozen tiger sharks moving peacefully with the rest of the pack as though they had been mildly sedated or were merely biding their time, waiting to attack.

"So where's the kraken?" Shane shouted.

"Would you believe, you're looking at it?" Christine said.

Nick and everyone on the tour stared into the glass. All he saw was the coral reef and the fish swimming mindlessly in a circle.

"There's no kraken," a young boy hollered.

"What a jip," a woman griped.

"Please be patient!" Christine said.

"Shane, what are you doing?" Bob yelled.

Nick turned and saw Shane slipping under the handrail. He rushed over and began banging on the glass. "Hey, kraken! You in there?"

"Young man, step back!" Christine shouted. "Do not pound on the—"

A gigantic tentacle suddenly appeared and would have grabbed Shane if it weren't for the thick glass. The appendage was thirty feet long if not more with suction cups the size of hubcaps. Each cup broadened as it adhered tighter to the glass, increasing the suction.

Nick was afraid it was going to break the glass. He grabbed Meg's arm and they took a step back. He watched as parts of the coral reef began to transform slowly into a humongous octopus.

"Oh my God, Nick," Meg said.

"That's so cool," Gabe said.

"Everyone let me present *Enteroctopus dofleini*, a giant Pacific octopus or what we call the kraken," Christine said.

"Wait a minute," Shane said. "Isn't a kraken a giant squid?"

"The myth suggests so, yes. But, the word *krake* is German for octopus. So you decide. Which would you choose?"

Nobody was up for a debate; they were too enthralled gawking at the monstrous creature staring back at them. Nick could only see one of its eyes. It was huge with a horizontal pupil.

"This large marine animal is a cephalopod, a Greek term meaning *head-feet* as the arms are attached to the head."

"Don't you mean tentacles?" Shane said.

"An octopus has arms as the suckers run all the way down the length of the appendage. Tentacles only have a single sucker at the tip. This particular species has 240 suction cups on each arm, and with eight arms that's a total of 1,920 suckers. Sometimes when an octopus gets hungry or bored, it might even eat one of its arms."

"That's crazy," Gabe said.

"It might sound crazy, but octopi have the same rejuvenating abilities as a lizard that loses it tail: it just grows back a new one."

"Oh my," a woman gasped.

Christine went on to say, "As you've just witnessed this octopus can change the pigmentation of its skin to blend in with its environment, acting as a camouflage."

"Sure fooled us," Bob said to Nick.

"I'll say."

"This creature is nearly 50 feet long and weighs 2,000 pounds. It has the capability of speeds of up to 25 miles per hour by pulling water through its mantle and ejecting the water through a siphon creating jet propulsion. It can also squirt out an ink smoke screen whenever it feels threatened."

"Wow," someone said.

Christine continued and asked, "Does everyone see the beak?"

Nick leaned on the handrail to get a better look. He thought only birds had beaks, but then he saw the mollusk-shaped mouth. "How do they eat?" he asked Christine.

"They have a paralytic and digestive toxin in their salivary glands that enables them to eat just about anything."

"Can they survive out of water?" a young woman asked.

"They can, but only for a short period of time. Here's an interesting note, as octopi are soft-bodied animals they're capable of squeezing through very narrow openings just as long as they are not smaller than the beak, which is the only hard part of its body."

"Kind of like a rat," Bob said.

"Yes, but an octopus is more intelligent than a rat, I assure you. Our marine biologist and zookeepers can attest to that. They've even given it a nickname."

"What's that?" Meg asked.

"Einstein. Which brings us to our demonstration," Christine said. She turned to a speaker pad on the wall and pushed a button. "We're ready."

A door to the left opened and a woman walked out. She was wearing a brown shirt and khakis. She came over and stood next to Christine.

"Hi, everyone. My name's Tilly O'Brien. I'm both a marine biologist and one of many zookeepers staffing this facility. As I am sure Christine has already mentioned, our resident giant Pacific octopus, which we fondly call Einstein, is quite the smart boy."

"How so?" Shane asked skeptically.

"Just watch." Tilly went over to a standup podium where a laptop computer was set up. She typed on the keypad.

Nick watched as a fifty-five gallon drum, suspended by a cable, dropped down into the aquarium from above. The top was sealed with a screw on lid similar to a childproof cap on a medicine bottle.

Tilly went up to the glass and gazed at the giant octopus. The colossal creature saw the woman and moved closer to the glass. "As you can see, Einstein has a knack for recognizing faces and knows who I am. You might even say we've become quite good friends. He also knows that I have a treat for him. But if he wants it, he's going to have to work for it."

"What's inside the drum?" Nick asked.

"It's full of krill, Einstein's favorite."

"Isn't the drum sealed?"

"It is. That's the test. Let's see if Einstein can figure it out." Tilly faced the glass and watched along with the rest of the tour group.

The giant octopus spotted the offering and propelled over to the drum. It wrapped the tip of one of its arms around the container and held it firmly with its suction cups. It gripped the lid with another arm and began to twist the cover.

"That's incredible," Nick said. "It's unscrewing the cap."

Everyone watched as the top came off—a cable with some slack was attached to the inside of the lid so it wouldn't drift away—and brown krill floated out.

The octopus greedily sucked up the crustaceans.

Once the ravenous creature was finished, the drum was hoisted back up and out of sight.

Christine thanked Tilly for the demonstration and motioned for everyone to follow her to the nearest exit.

"That was really something," Nick said to Meg as they shuffled out.

"Finally, something positive for your report."

"Let's hope it keeps up."

# 9

## SEA MONSTER COVE

Nick and Meg were the last ones to come out of the aquarium. As soon as Christine saw them, she said to the rest of the group, "Well, I hope you enjoyed the Tank." A few people commented that they had.

"What's the next exhibit called?" Nick asked.

"You'll see, it's just up there," Christine said, pointing to the flagstone pathway sloping up a hummock covered with artificial turf.

It was an easy stroll up the hillock and only took a couple of minutes. A large sign was posted at the top: SEA MONSTER COVE.

As soon as Nick passed by the sign he realized that the hillside was the backside for rows of elevated bleachers that looked down on a body of murky water with a small island in the center. A cave was tucked back from a sandy beach.

Christine stood on a platform, directing everyone to sit in the front row of the bleachers, which was roughly thirty feet above the water.

Nick noticed a rippling effect as the water sloshed against the sides of the high surrounding concrete retaining wall and on the shore near the cave that was cut into a landscape of artificial rock. The motion was like a whirlpool, which meant that something very big was swimming around the island beneath the surface.

"Welcome to Sea Monster Cove," Christine said. "If you look closely, you might catch a glimpse of Caddy."

"What's Caddy?" Nick asked.

"She's a cadborosaurus. Our sea serpent."

Nick kept his eyes on the water until he saw a long shape under the surface. It had a long neck and flippers, and was the length of a small whale. He could tell by the murmurings that others had spotted it as well.

"Where in the world did you find that?" Meg asked Christine, after spotting the sea creature.

"Off the coast of British Columbia."

"You mean these things actually exist?" Nick asked.

"Seeing is believing, right?"

"That isn't real!" Shane said. "It's like that mechanical shark at Universal Studios, the one that was in *Jaws*."

"I'm going to have to agree with my son," Bob said.

"Oh, it's real, I assure you." Christine walked over to a glass holding tank set up on the platform, filled with two-foot long fish. A chute was under a sealed opening in the side of the glass and extended ten feet out over the cove.

Christine grabbed a handle and lifted the plate on the side of the tank, releasing some water and a few of the fish before closing it. The freed fish slid down to the end of the chute and flew into the air.

The sea serpent burst out of the water. It had a horse-like head and an extremely long neck. It opened its gigantic mouth, scooped up the feeder fish in midair then slammed back down into the water, splashing the platform and some of the visitors.

"Jesus, did you see that?" Bob said.

"I have to say, that looked real to me," Nick answered back.

"They actually captured that thing?" Meg said to Nick.

"Must have. That's truly unbelievable."

"While we let Caddy enjoy her little snack, I would like to direct everyone's attention to the beach area. Does everyone see our zookeeper?"

Nick saw a young man standing by the cave entrance.

"Everyone, let's all wave to Cam," Christine said. The group did as instructed.

Cam waved back. He turned and walked inside the cave. A few seconds passed before he came out, followed by what looked like a miniature brontosaurus with a long neck and tail and was five feet taller than Cam. Three more identical looking creatures came out of the cave and they all gathered at an embankment covered with white-blossomed liana and began chomping on the foliage like cattle grazing on a pasture.

"These docile creatures are sauropods also known as mokele-mbemebe."

"My God, you found dinosaurs?" Meg said.

"That's right."

"But from where?" Nick asked, totally blown away.

"The Congo River Basin."

"How much does one of those weigh?"

"Close to 1,000 pounds."

"How come we've never heard of them?" Bob asked.

"That's because they've never really existed until now."

"What's that supposed to mean?"

"I'll explain later. In tomorrow's tour."

Nick checked his watch. It was a few minutes before six. He noticed that the stadium lights were not as bright. As it was approaching dusk outside the dome he figured that the same condition was being simulated inside to conserve power as everything was run on solar energy.

"Before we return to the hotel," Christine said, "I would like to introduce you all to Patrick."

"Who's Patrick?" Gabe asked.

Nick heard a woman gasp. He turned and saw a hideous blob creep across the platform. "What the hell is that?" he blurted, unable to contain himself.

"Patrick is what's known as a globster."

"A what?"

"Have you ever gone to the beach and found something dead that has washed ashore and wondered what it was?"

"Sure. One time we found a jellyfish in some kelp and wasn't so sure what it was at first."

"Well, that's Patrick—the mysterious carcass."

"This is a joke, right?" Nick said. He glanced back at the thing on the platform. It was gray and slimy and had a strange glob face with two deep-socket eyeholes and a puckered mouth. The bizarre abomination had only two stubby front legs with webbed feet. It dragged itself toward Christine. The tour guide grabbed a pole that was leaning against the fish tank and used it to keep Patrick at bay.

"But how is it alive if it's dead?" Meg asked.

"Like I said, that's the mystery."

"What happens if you touch it?" Shane asked.

"I wouldn't recommend doing that," Christine said.

"Why's that?" Nick asked.

"And that concludes our tour for today." Christine drew everyone's attention to the exit path at the end of the bleachers and stood by as the tour group got up to leave.

Nick didn't know if Christine had purposely ignored his question or simply hadn't heard him.

By the time they reached the pool area of the hotel, the dome had completely darkened. Lights came on around the hotel and the swimming pool and along the walkways.

"I'm a little hungry, how about you?" Meg asked Nick.

"I don't know, after seeing that thing."

"That was *definitely* creepy."

"Spooky is more like it."

# 10

## NIGHT OWL

After freshening up in their rooms, Nick's family and Bob's all met down at the lobby for dinner. This time when they went to the dining room there was a hostess to greet them and escort them to their table.

As soon as Nick sat down, he noticed that a screen partition had been drawn across the far wall, discreetly blocking off the buffet counter. Two bottles of complimentary wine and glasses were in the center of the table.

He picked up a bottle and inspected the label. "Anyone for Chardonnay?"

"Please," Meg said and picked up a wineglass.

"I'd like some," Rhonda said.

Nick looked at Bob, but he was already pouring himself a glass from the other bottle, which was a red wine.

"Well, this is a step up from lunch," Bob said, taking a sip from his glass.

"Should we toast?" Nick said.

"What about us?" Shane whined. "Don't we get some?"

Gabe gave his father an expectant look.

Nick glanced around the dining room at the other patrons. No one seemed to be interested in what they were doing, as they were too busy socializing amongst themselves or eating their meals. "Sure, why not. But just half a glass."

Meg gave him a look, but she didn't object.

Once the wines were poured, Nick raised his glass. "To the most weirdest vacation ever!"

"And it's only just started," Bob said with a laugh.

Everyone clinked their glasses together.

A waiter came to their table with menus and explained the specials of the day.

The service turned out to be impeccable, so much, that Nick felt guilty after he'd finished his meal he wasn't able to show his appreciation and give the waiter a big fat tip as there was no bill, everything being paid for by the company.

"I brought along a malt scotch if anyone's interested," Bob said.

"All right Dad!" Shane said.

"Sorry, son."

Shane frowned, but stayed quiet.

"Why don't we hang out on our balcony and have a few?" Bob said. "We have a great view of these trees."

"Really. Our room looks out over the pool." Nick turned to Meg. "Up for a drink?"

"Sure," Meg said.

They got up from the table and ambled through the dining room. Nick glanced out of a large picture window and saw some adults and kids swimming out in the pool and a young couple soaking in a Jacuzzi.

An elevator opened and guests stepped out. Nick and the others got in and rode the lift up to the fourth floor.

The Pascale's suite was conveniently located next to the ice machine in the hallway. Bob opened the door to their room and everyone went inside. The layout was similar to Nick and Meg's room. Bob handed Shane a white plastic bucket to fill with ice and also gave his son money to get soft drinks from the beverage machine.

When Shane returned with the sodas and ice, he and Gabe snuck off into their own room through the adjoining door connecting to the next suite.

"What are they doing in there if they don't have their phones or iPads?" Nick asked.

"There's a movie channel," Bob said, standing at a table, dumping ice cubes in their glasses. "Don't worry I checked it out first. Nothing R-rated."

"I'd hope not," Nick said. "This is supposed to be a family resort."

"Yeah, and who came up with this wacky place? Tim Burton?" Bob twisted the cap off the bottle of scotch and poured some into each of the glasses. He handed Meg and Rhonda their drinks then gave Nick his glass.

Bob opened the sliding glass door to the patio area for Meg and Rhonda. They went over to the padded lounge chairs, put their drinks on a small glass table between them, and sat on the cushions.

Nick walked over to the edge of the balcony to peer down over the railing, and almost bumped his head on a large pane of glass. He looked around and saw that the entire patio area was sealed in. "Nice to see they took precautions to make the balcony child safe."

"I don't think that's why they did it," Bob said, coming over and standing next to Nick.

"What do you mean?"

"I don't think the glass is meant to prevent someone from falling over the edge. It was designed to keep something from getting in. That's one-inch thick double pane glass. The same kind they use for glass enclosures at zoos."

"Well, this is a zoo."

"Yeah, so what's out there?" Bob went in and switched off all the lights, eliminating the reflecting glare of the mirrored image of the interior of the suite.

It took a moment for Nick's eyes to adjust to the gloomy outside and soon he began to make out the shapes of trees. The canopy stretched high above the hotel. He could see shadows moving between the branches.

A large shape swooped right across the front of the glass.

Nick jumped back and spilt his drink on his shirt. "Jesus, did you see that?"

Bob had turned away briefly and Meg and Rhonda had been too busy talking to each other so no one noticed. The three gawked at Nick.

"Whatever it was, it was huge!" Nick said.

The women got up from their chairs to get a closer look.

Bob pressed his face against the glass to peer outside.

Rhonda screamed and Meg yelled out, "Oh my God!"

"Jesus, Nick," Bob said, half laughing. "What the hell is that?"

Nick watched the creature hovering a foot away from the glass.

It had a wingspan of about six feet with three talon claws on the front of each wing like a bat or a pterodactyl's, though it looked more like a giant owl as its small rounded head, short body, and wings were covered with gray feathers. It had gangly legs that bent back at the knees like a human, and four-toed feet.

Strangely, it had no beak or any nasal passages. Instead, it had an O shaped mouth that looked like it was about to wrap its lips around the end of a garden hose.

The eyes were the most alarming things about the creature, as they glowed bright red like two taillights on the back of a car.

"Is that thing eerie or what?" Bob said.

"What in God's name is that?" Meg asked.

"Damned if I know," Nick replied.

"I'm going back inside," Rhonda said and took her drink into the room.

Nick could see his reflection in the window haloed in red from the glow of the creature's eyes. He had a weird sensation, like a tight cap had just been placed over his brain. He could feel pressure building up behind his eyes. It was as if something was pulling at his subconscious.

"Honey, are you okay?"

Nick thought he heard a voice but couldn't be completely sure as his head was swimming...

His shoulders were violently shaken. Nick jerked his head like he'd been slapped and saw Bob staring at him with a bewildered look on his face.

"Snap out of it, man," Bob said, releasing Nick's shoulders.

"What just happened?" Nick looked down at his drink in his hand and saw that most of it had spilled out on the deck.

"I think that thing was playing mind games with your head."

Nick stepped back like he might fall over and flopped down on the chair Rhonda had been sitting in. Meg grabbed his glass from his hand before he dropped it.

"Should we get a doctor?" Meg asked.

"No. Give me a sec." Nick closed his eyes and took a deep breath. He leaned forward and rocked back and forth.

"What's going on?" Rhonda asked, rushing onto the patio.

"We're not sure," Bob said.

"I'm okay," Nick said. He sat back in the chair and opened his eyes. He put out his hand and Meg handed him back his near-empty tumbler.

"Do you have a headache?" Meg asked.

"No, nothing like that," Nick said, rubbing his temple with his fingertips. "It's hard to explain. I'm fine now."

"Guys care for another round?" Bob asked.

"Sure," Nick said. He downed the rest of his drink and handed Bob his glass.

"I'm still good." Meg raised her glass and showed Bob. He gave her a nod and shuffled into the suite.

"What did that thing do to you?" Meg asked.

"I have no idea."

"This place is really starting to freak me out."

"You and me both," Nick said and looked out the glass.

He was relieved to see that the creature was gone.

# 11

## THE AVIARY

After another bland breakfast at the buffet, Christine had everyone muster in the lobby for the next tour. As the observation deck was on the fifth floor of the hotel and there were twenty people in the tour group, she opted to take the stairs rather than split everyone up taking the elevator.

Nick and Meg took up the rear following Bob and Rhonda and the others up the stairwell. Gabe and Shane were somewhere up ahead and had developed a bond, enjoying the freedom of having their own room, which seemed to make the teenagers more tolerable to be around, even when they were forced to spend so much time with their parents.

"At least we get to walk off that grand breakfast," Nick joked as they reached the landing for the second floor and kept going up.

"My Belgian waffle was like rubber," Meg said. "I don't get it. If they can serve such a wonderful dinner, why not the breakfast?"

They reached the third floor and trudged past the fire door to the next level.

Nick could hear a heavyset man higher up, panting, and struggling up the stairs, sounding like he was on the verge of having a coronary and knew the guy would surely slam Christine's decision not to use the elevator on his evaluation.

When they finally reached the fifth floor, Christine held the fire door open so everyone could pass through onto the observation deck, which was completely glassed in.

Once everyone was inside, Christine walked up and gazed out through the massive window that looked out over an area of tall trees inside a giant enclosure of stainless steel netting supported by long cables attached to the underside of the dome's girded ceiling.

"This is day two of our tour. If you would please spread out, there should be enough room for everyone to get a good view of our next attraction—the Aviary."

"What's so special about it?" Bob asked. "I think we've all seen exotic birds one time or another."

"Not like these you haven't."

Nick spotted what he thought was a Cessna flying between the trees. It had a wingspan of 18 feet and soared through the air like a glider. The giant bird landed on a thick bough fifty feet above the ground. Perched on the limb, it stood about twelve feet tall. The head and beak were sleek like an eagle.

"Look at the size of that thing," a woman said.

"I've never seen a bird that big," Nick said. "What is it?"

"That's a thunderbird." Christine looked around then pointed. "If you look over there, you'll see another one in those trees."

"Where in the world did you find them?" Meg asked.

"Here."

"In the United States?"

"You could say that."

Nick watched the giant bird open its enormous wings and dive off the branch toward the observation deck. It came so close to the window, the wingtips actually swept across the glass, making everyone jump back.

Just like last night when Nick had seen the shadowy shape flash by Bob's balcony. It had to have been a thunderbird.

"How would everyone like to get a closer look?" Christine asked. At first there were no takers, then Shane piped up, "Sure. Do we get to ride one of those things?"

"I'm not too sure that would be advisable as thunderbirds are birds of prey and are quite unpredictable. But if you think the thunderbirds are impressive, wait till you see what else resides in the Aviary." Christine led the way to a glass door that opened up to an enclosed pedestrian bridge, which extended halfway into the free flight cage and came to a dead end on a massive granite column.

Nick noticed that some of the people were apprehensive and hesitated for a moment before entering the elevated corridor. He quickly learned why when it was his turn.

The walkway was also made of glass.

It was like stepping out into thin air.

He looked at his shoes and the vegetation all the way down to the ground. He got a hollow sensation in his stomach and experienced vertigo for a second.

"I think I'm going to be sick," Meg said, glancing at her feet.

"Don't look down and you'll be fine," Nick said, walking alongside and putting his arm around her back.

Christine signaled for everyone to stop and look out the right side of the pedestrian walkway.

Ten creatures with fox-like faces were dangling upside down, wrapped in black cloaks, suspended by a single toe hooked to the steel mesh netting.

"What are they?" a woman asked.

"Those are ahools," Christine said.

"Did you say a-holes?" Shane poked Gabe and they both started giggling.

"Shane, behave," Rhonda told her son.

"No, I said ahools," Christine said calmly even though it was apparent she was getting a little irritated by Shane's juvenile jokes. "They're a megabat from Java in Indonesia. They got their name because they make a *hoooh* sound when they call to one another."

"I thought bats slept in caves and hunted at night?" Nick asked, wondering why these animals were sleeping out in broad daylight even though it was synthetic lighting inside the dome.

"Each of these bats weighs about thirty pounds and because of their astoundingly large bodies no longer have the ability to transmit echolocation pulses. Which means they are no longer nocturnal predators and hunt during the day."

"Boring," Shane said. "So why aren't they hunting now?" He slapped the glass with both hands. "Hey! Wake up!"

"Shane, I'm not going to tell you again..." but then Rhonda stopped when she saw what was happening outside.

"Good God," Nick said. One of the giant bats had unfurled its wings. Dangling upside down by its feet, the creature spread its enormous wings brushing up against the others and rousting them awake.

"I would suggest everyone step away from the glass," Christine warned.

Suddenly, there was a flurry of wings and the ahools flew at the enclosed walkway. They bared their fangs and clawed at the glass. Nick was afraid they would smash their way in with their heavy bodies.

A young girl screamed. Her mother turned her away so she wouldn't have to see the monstrous bats.

"How do they even know we're in here?" Nick yelled to be heard over the clamoring outside. "What's the old saying, blind as a bat?"

"I'm afraid ahools have excellent eyesight," Christine said. "But they are easily distracted. If everyone would remain still and be quiet, I'm sure something will get their attention and draw them away."

Meg whispered to Nick, "Did you see that poor little girl? She was really scared."

"Yeah. Not exactly what you would call a fun place."

Just as Christine had predicted, a small flock of pigeons flew by that were probably a food source for the predators, and the ahools gave pursuit.

Another bird-like creature soared by.

"Hey, Bob. Didn't that look like that owl thing from last night?" Nick asked his friend.

"Yeah, it did."

"That was a mothman," Christine said, obviously overhearing the two speaking.

Nick instantly thought of the Richard Gere movie he'd seen years ago called *The Mothman Prophecies* but never remembered seeing such a creature. He did recall that the film had something to do with foreseeing the future as Gere's character was mysteriously drawn to a bridge where he saved a woman when the structure collapsed.

He wondered if he might have been affected in the same way.

"If you'll all follow me to the end of the footbridge," Christine said. "I'd like to show you more of our spectacular birds."

Meg got Nick's attention. "Where are they finding these creatures? I've never heard of thunderbirds or those giant bats?"

"Good question. Want me to ask?"

"Sure."

"Christine?"

The tour guide turned and faced Nick. "Yes?"

"Did someone go out and capture these creatures?"

"In essence, yes. But we'll get to that later."

"Always with the *later*," Meg whispered to Nick.

Christine stopped and pointed down at a small pond where a giant black bird with a four-foot long red beak was wallowing in the water. It looked to be about 6 feet tall and had a wingspan of 12 feet. "The species you are looking at is a kongamatok, which translates to "breaker of boats" as these legendary creatures were notorious for attacking African fishermen in their canoes."

"You said *legendary*?" Nick questioned.

"That's right."

"Care to elaborate?"

"Later," Christine said.

"I'm telling you, I'm going to wring her neck," Meg whispered harshly into Nick's ear.

"And that concludes our visit to the Aviary." Christine motioned for everyone to turn around and head back down the pedestrian bridge toward the hotel.

She hung back and waited for Nick and Meg. "I know I've been evasive answering some of your questions and I do apologize, but I've been given explicit instructions not to divulge such information until the next leg of our tour. I hope you understand. Besides, our scientists can better explain."

"Scientists?" Meg said.

"Yes, the brilliant minds that created these creatures."

# 12

## LITTLE SHOP OF HORRORS

Christine led them out of the hotel and down an aggregate path past the pool toward a large circular building.

Nick saw two other groups of at least thirty people, each going their separate ways, one toward the Tank and the other up the hill to Sea Monster Cove. He glanced over his right shoulder at the massive net screen covering the bird habitat. Looking straight ahead, he could see higher structures behind the building they were about to enter, deep inside the dome.

He gazed up at the bold lettering over the entrance.

BIOENGINEERING LABORATORY AND ANIMATRONICS
WORKSHOP COMPLEX.

As soon as everyone was inside, Christine escorted her party through the foyer to an open doorway of a small auditorium the size of a college classroom with five tiered rows of seats and sitting capacity for fifty people.

Nick and Meg followed Bob, Rhonda, and the boys up to the third row so they would have a good view of the stage in the front of the room. A lectern and a table were set up next to a white projector screen.

A woman in her thirties and an older looking man with a scruffy beard, wearing white lab coats, stood by the podium.

Two men were on the other side of the stage. They were ruggedly dressed in brown shirts, khakis, and hiking boots. The taller man had blond hair and was lean and muscular. The man next to him was Hispanic and huskily built.

Nick could tell by their weathered faces they spent much of their time in the great outdoors.

"Hello, everyone," said the woman in the white lab coat. "My name is Professor Nora Howard." She turned to the man next to her. "This is

Dr. Joel McCabe. He is our head geneticist and is in charge of the bioengineering lab." She waited for the doctor to acknowledge everyone. He gave a curt nod as if being there was a complete waste of his time and there was somewhere else he'd rather be.

Nick took an instant disliking to the person.

Professor Howard turned to the other two men and said, "These gentlemen are Jack Tremens and Miguel Walla. If it weren't for Jack and Miguel, this zoo would not be possible."

Dr. McCabe frowned, taking offense to that statement while Jack and Miguel both smiled at the professor.

"For the past three years, Jack and Miguel have traveled all over the world, and in many cases risked their lives, searching and finding the most dangerous and elusive creatures on the planet. Cryptozoology, or what is known as the study of "hidden animals" has always been a pseudoscience not recognized by the scientific community as there has never been substantiating evidence that cryptids have ever existed except in myths and folklore. But that is no longer true. They do exist. Right here."

Nick saw Bob raise his hand.

"Yes?" Professor Howard said.

"So you're saying these two men captured that sea serpent and those giant birds and those dinosaur looking things?"

Jack stepped forward to field the question. "I'm afraid Nora...I mean Professor Howard, gives Miguel and I far too much credit. Yes, we have been able to catch a few of these creatures but in most cases, we're lucky if we can retrieve a hair fiber."

"Which is all we need," Dr. McCabe piped in, cutting Jack off. "Seeing as almost every creature here is a byproduct of our bioengineering program."

"So you're saying, you made those things in your laboratory?"

Nick couldn't help thinking that Bob was starting to sound like a heckler.

"Human babies are conceived in laboratories through stem cell research, why not these creatures?" Professor Howard said and put up her hand. "But before we get ahead of ourselves, perhaps we should take a few minutes and watch a video we have prepared for you that will better explain everything."

Jack went over and dimmed the lights while Professor Howard stepped up to the lectern and turned on the video player that operated the overhead projector attached to the ceiling near the back of the small auditorium.

Nick sat back in his chair as the film began on the projector screen with a brief introduction promoting Wilde Enterprises. The voice of the narrator sounded a lot like Morgan Freeman who then began speaking about the hereditary material in all organisms known as deoxyribonucleic acid or DNA. The tutorial had basic illustrations and was easy to understand, geared primarily for a young audience.

He watched as a double helix rotated on the screen and certain strands were removed from the pattern and new colored strands were inserted to take their place thus altering the DNA.

Once that segment was over, the presentation discussed the process of cloning, primarily organism cloning, a procedure of creating new multicellular organisms.

Nick looked away from the screen for a split second and saw Dr. McCabe sneak off and slip out the door.

From there the film went on to the case study of Dolly the sheep, the first mammal to be successfully cloned from an adult somatic cell, a tedious endeavor that took scientists 434 attempts before attaining a viable embryo. Nick wondered how many tries were taken to create a cryptid creature; a thousand times, ten thousand, more?

The movie segued into a short cartoon showing the conceptual process of creating a cryptid, beginning in the test tube. The test subject quickly evolved into a cuddly baby bigfoot. The toddler's antics were comical to watch as it took its first steps, making the children squeal with delight and the parents laugh each time it took a pratfall. The bigfoot got even cuter as the progression was sped up to adulthood making the animated cartoon character seem harmless and goofy.

Nick worried the presentation was sugarcoating the possible dangers associated with creating such a creature so children would not be alarmed. He looked around the room until he spotted the little girl that had been frightened by the giant bats in the Aviary. She was laughing, enjoying the cartoon and didn't seem to be suffering any emotional scars from her earlier scare. Kids could be so resilient.

The video droned on for another minute before concluding with the narrator hoping everyone enjoyed the presentation before signing off.

Nick looked over at Meg and saw her eyelids drooping. Sitting in the dark room was making him sleepy as well. He leaned in and whispered in her ear, "Wake up," and her eyes popped open.

Jack turned up the lights.

Professor Howard looked at the clock on the wall. "We have a couple of minutes before your tour continues if there is anyone that would like to come up and ask questions."

Shane and Gabe made their way to the end of the row and down the steps to the front of the room. They went up to Jack and Miguel and began chatting them up as if they were famous action/adventure movie stars on the red carpet, signing autographs.

The boys seemed genuinely excited. Jack was taking a special interest, and by the way he was gesticulating, was telling them about one of their escapades.

Nick couldn't help but feel a little jealous. Even though he was proud of what he did for a living, working a mundane job in the relatively safe marketing department was a far cry from risking one's life, gallivanting all over the world in search of exotic animals.

"Did you see the way Jack Tremens was looking at Professor Howard?" Meg asked.

"What about it?" Nick replied.

"I think they're an item."

"You do, huh?"

Christine waved for everyone to follow her out of the auditorium. Nick was expecting the professor and the other two men to come along thinking they would be accompanying the group for the tour of the bioengineering laboratory but they remained behind. He quickly learned why when Christine announced that no one was allowed inside the lab except for the research team.

A few people voiced their disappointment while the rest were content just standing in the corridor and peering into the laboratory through the large pane windows.

Dr. McCabe and two lab assistants were busily at work and ignored the group of visitors gawking at them from the other side of the glass.

Before Nick was promoted to the marketing department he'd been a purchasing agent in procurement, ordering various supplies and equipment for a medical division of Wilde Enterprises, so he was familiar with many of the laboratory instruments and machines.

Some of the workstations in the back of the room were cluttered with Bunsen burners, racks of test tubes, beakers, and flasks while the benches closest to the viewing windows were kept neat and were mostly bare. A table and a few chairs were in a corner for impromptu meetings as there were scientific notations scribbled on a white board on an easel stand and anatomic charts posted on the wall.

Nick heard a screech inside the lab.

Dr. McCabe immediately stopped what he was doing and rushed across the lab. One of the lab assistants started to follow but the other man shook his head and they returned to their work.

"Did you hear that?" Meg asked.

"Sounded like some kind of animal," Nick responded.

They watched as the doctor went to the back of the lab. He leaned down behind a counter so it was impossible to see what he was doing. Nick saw the doctor's hand come up then down like he was striking something.

The odd cry stopped.

Dr. McCabe stood and walked back to where he had been previously at work.

"That was strange," Meg said.

"There's something not right about that guy," Nick said. "You don't think he's some kind of Dr. Moreau?"

"What, you think he creates these things just so he can abuse them?"

"It's a possibility."

"If you'll all follow me," Christine said in a loud voice and walked everyone down to another part of the building.

A sign was over two double doors: ANIMATRONIC WORKSHOP.

Christine pushed through the doors, which swung open into a large workshop. A small crew of three men and two women were working on different projects.

An artist was sitting at her drawing board while a sculptor stood at a nearby table, copying the sketch and creating a similar creature out of clay that looked like a giant lizard.

A welder was finishing up with a humanoid skeletal frame that stood eight feet high. The woman removed her face shield to inspect the joints.

One man was operating a joystick on a control box and testing the motor functions on a large puppet that looked exactly like the giant bats they'd seen in the Aviary.

There were tables everywhere with dismantled body parts and busts of creatures' heads and torsos. A work-in-progress bigfoot was partially covered with a head and furry torso, the arms and legs still bare metal. The place looked like a demonic child's playroom after all the toys had been torn apart.

A man with a white goatee and gray hair pulled back in a ponytail was inspecting a full size replicate of a mokele-mbemebe which looked exactly like one of the sauropods from Sea Monster Cove. He turned and gave everyone a warm smile.

Nick was completely blown away. It was Burt Owen, the legendary wizard responsible for creating the most outlandish special effects in so many horror and science fiction movies. He was right up there with make-up artists Stan Winston, Dick Smith, and Rob Bottin.

Gabe was also a big fan.

The special effects on the last two films that Nick had taken Gabe to see had been by Burt Owen whose team had created the gigantic insects in the films *The Next World* and *Battleground Earth*, and for which he was being nominated for Oscars in the Special Make-Up category.

Owen introduced himself and talked a little about how the industry had changed through the years from time-lapse photography and using stop-motion miniatures, evolving into the technologies of computer generated imagery and the artistry of building full-size animatronics that actors could actually interact with, instead of performing to projections on a blue screen.

"Have you all been to Sea Monster Cove?" Owen asked.

"We went there yesterday," Nick said. He glanced around and saw most of the group nodding their heads.

"Then I'm sure you saw this little beauty," Owen said. He placed his hand on the sauropod's shoulder and gave it a loving pat like it was his pet and was real. He looked up at the dinosaur's head at the end of the long neck, five feet above his own.

"What, you're saying those things are all robots?" Shane said.

"Heavens no," Owen laughed. "Before this facility was even built, Carter Wilde asked if I would be interested in creating models for his bioengineering team. Most of the creatures you have seen so far were designed by my company and are just a blueprint for the real ones."

Owen called one of his technicians over to assist him. The man had shoulder length hair and wore a tie dye T-shirt and jeans. He went over to a table and grabbed a control box with a long cable attached to a receptacle under the sauropod's belly. He pushed a button and began maneuvering a series of toggle switches.

Everyone in the tour group was startled when the dinosaur swiveled its head on its long neck and took a step forward, swishing its long tail across the floor and nearly sweeping Owen off his feet.

"Careful there, Ray," Owen said to the technician.

"Sorry about that, Burt. The controls are a little twitchy." The operator kept manipulating the levers.

The sauropod opened its mouth and bellowed.

Nick couldn't believe how real it seemed. The facial expressions it made, the detailed craftsmanship of every aspect of its body, the fluid movements of the neck and legs, even that realistic roar it made.

"How many of these zoo creatures have you made?" Nick asked.

"A few."

"So how do we tell the fakes from the real ones?" Shane asked.

Owen gave Shane a snide look and grinned. "You can't."

# 13

## BIPED HABITAT

The tour group broke for lunch and returned to the hotel. Again, the restaurant was set up buffet-style like breakfast. This time the cuisine was Mexican.

Nick had a couple of soft tacos and a plate of rice and beans. He was pleased to find cold bottled beers in a tub of ice at the end of the line and grabbed himself a Modelo.

There was a basket of tortilla chips and a bowl of salsa waiting for them at their table. Meg had the chili relleno casserole; Gabe a big plate of enchiladas and chicken quesadillas.

Bob, Rhonda, and Shane had sat at a separate table so that the two families could share some quality time together with their sons.

Nick was glad Gabe was having a good time and that Shane's sour disposition hadn't rubbed off on his boy. Gabe was excited that he could meet Burt Owen and talked a lot about the animatronics workshop. Now that he'd had a behind-the-scenes experience and seen how some of the special effects make-up was done, he was even more enthusiastic about the movie magic responsible for creating the monsters for the big screen.

After washing down his meal with the last of his beer, Nick had to admit that lunch hadn't been half bad. He was feeling so good, he planned to give the meal a favorable review.

Once everyone had been given the opportunity to go to the restroom, they assembled out by the pool.

Christine escorted the group down a wide walkway between the Bioengineering Laboratory and Animatronics Workshop Complex and the Aviary to another orbicular building almost flush with the sloping wall of the dome.

Nick gazed up at the name over the entrance—BIPED HABITAT— as they stepped inside.

A long hallway stretched to the center of the building and opened up into a large circular atrium with a skylight high above. The light shining down was the only illumination in the room. Nick glanced around and saw that the curved wall surrounding them was made of opaque glass.

Christine waited for everyone to gather around. "Welcome to Biped Habitat. As suggested by the name, this facility houses our two-legged cryptids."

"You actually caught a sasquatch?" Shane asked.

"In a matter of speaking, yes."

"This I have to see," Nick said to Meg. This time Nick and Meg were directly behind Christine. Bob, Rhonda, Shane, and Gabe were following just ahead of the tour group.

Nick noticed as they walked, lights would start to come on, illuminating the space on the other side of the glass wall that a moment ago appeared to be a solid mass. It reminded Nick of whenever he would go into the grocery store and went down the aisles with the upright refrigeration units, which would be dark inside to conserve energy then would light up as soon as a person approached and opened the door to take something out.

"There are five separate habitats in this building," Christine said. "Each habitat measures twenty feet on the front glass then extends back for sixty feet in a pie wedge floor plan to an eighty-foot back wall and are individually regulated with the proper climate control suited for each species."

Everyone bunched together so they could all see inside the first habitat. A small area of redwoods and sequoia pines stretched up to the ceiling and reminded Nick of the Pacific Northwest. A fine mist drifted down from the ceiling simulating fog. Shrubs and ferns were positioned around the trees. There were a few boulders but Nick could tell they weren't real and made of Fiberglas.

On the back wall was a giant mural of a majestic mountain range, crags and peaks jutting onto a canvas of sky blue and fluffy white clouds.

Meg tapped Nick on the arm. "There's something just behind that tree by the big rock."

Nick watched as the creature lumbered out from behind the trees.

"Oh my God!" a woman gasped. Other people shared her same reaction.

The bigfoot was eight feet tall, stocky, with dark-gray fur covering most of its body, its broad shoulders massive like a suited-up NFL lineman. Its brawny arms were husky like its thickset legs. A full mane of hair covered the top of its head and both sides of its cheekbones, forming a short beard under its chin. The humanoid face looked to have a permanent scowl with its furrowed brow, large deep-set eyes, and thin-lipped mouth.

Each hand was unbelievably huge. Nick could see the bigfoot easily palming a heavy medicine ball like he often saw basketball players do on the court.

The bigfoot glared back at everyone through the glass.

"Is it me, or does he looked pissed," Nick whispered to Meg.

"Certainly not glad to see *us*," Meg replied.

Another bigfoot ventured from behind a tree trunk, squatted in front of a bush and began picking berries off of the branches.

"Of course I'm sure you all recognize these creatures as the North American bigfoot, often called sasquatch. Each one of these creatures stands eight feet tall and weighs roughly 600 pounds."

"Did Jack and Miguel capture them?" Gabe asked.

"Not exactly. They were able to bring back a hair follicle they found in the forest. These bigfoot were bioengineered by Dr. McCabe."

"So they're not real?" Shane said.

"Sure they are," Christine responded. "Each one of these creature's DNA has been exactly coded to that fiber of hair. Believe me, they're the real deal. Shall we continue?"

The next habitat resembled a snowcapped mountain ridge with a large cave carved in the side of the rock. A fan was blowing snowflakes about the enclosure.

Nick noticed a thermometer fastened to the glass. The temperature was twenty degrees Fahrenheit.

Once everyone had moved into position and had a good view, Christine began by saying, "Here we have the legendary abominable snowman from the Himalayan region of Nepal. Often referred to as yeti."

Nick watched two yetis come out of the cave. They were not at all what he expected and looked nothing like the abominable snowman at the Matterhorn bobsled ride at Disneyland or the carnivorous ice creature from Star Wars.

They had long whitish fur and were extremely muscular, not as stocky as the bigfoot but slightly taller, and were identical in every way. Each yeti had narrow set eyes, a feline nose, pointy flesh toned ears, and a mouth that was constantly snarling, like the creature was ready to rip off somebody's head.

A couple of parents had pulled their children back away from the glass. Nick couldn't really blame them. These things were scary.

"Just to put everyone's minds at rest, only one of these yetis is real. The other one is an animatronic."

"Thank God," a woman said with relief and smiled sheepishly down at her young daughter.

"Oh yeah, which one?" a man blurted from the group. "They look the same to me."

Christine grinned at the man and gave him a playful shrug.

Burt Owen hadn't been exaggerating when he said that no one would be able to distinguish a bioengineered creature from an animatronic.

"This way," Christine said and everyone milled in front of the next exhibit. The habitat was a desert scene of sand and cacti. The overhead lights had been dimmed to simulate nightfall.

The red mercury ball on the temperature gauge was at 87 degrees.

"How many of you have ever heard of a chupacabra?" Christine asked the group.

Only three people raised their hands.

"Aren't they those creepy things that go around sucking other animal's blood?" Shane said.

"That's right. Normally found in Latin America and southern U.S. states like Texas and New Mexico. Chupacabra is Spanish for *goatsucker* as it drinks the blood of small livestock. Some say they're nothing more than mangy coyotes that feed on weak animals. But one thing is definitely true..." Christine paused, waiting for someone to take the bait.

Nick went in hook, line, and sinker. "What's that?"

"Chupacabras *are* vampires. They can hypnotize a prey by staring into its eyes, actually causing paralysis."

"Yeah, right!" Shane said. He pressed his face up to the glass and cupped his hands on either side of his head. "You sure they're in there? I don't see anything."

Christine looked over at a newly installed dimmer light switch on the wall that still needed some touchup paint around the plate.

"I should warn you, chupacabras can be a little frightening," Christine said. She waited as the parents prepared to shield their children's eyes if need be.

Christine turned the knob all the way and the entire habitat lit up.

Four hideous creatures were hunched over a goat lying on its side, kicking its hooves in the sand. The chupacabras snapped their heads up as soon as the lights came on. Their grotesque faces were smeared with blood. Each one slurped a long serpentine tongue back into its mouth. They were gaunt and stood about four feet tall and looked like giant skinned rats without any ears.

A little girl screamed.

Nick turned and saw it was the same girl that had been frightened by the giant bats in the Aviary. If the ahools didn't give her nightmares, the chupacabras certainly would.

"That is so disgusting," a woman said.

Christine quickly reached for the light switch. The habitat went pitch black.

"I am sorry," she apologized to everyone. "I forgot it was their feeding time."

"But that goat was alive," Meg said. "That's animal cruelty."

"I assure you our zookeepers treat all feeder animals humanely. If I can direct everyone's attention to the back of the habitat."

A light came on and a door opened up on the desert mural on the back wall of the sun setting on the horizon. A person stepped out.

It was the zookeeper, Cam, the sauropod wrangler from Sea Monster Cove.

He entered the small patch of light and disappeared into the dark enclosure. A couple of seconds later, he reappeared and was carrying the goat in his arms. He placed the goat on the ground in front of the open doorway, shooed it inside, and closed the door.

"See, the goat wasn't harmed. Think of it as donating at the Red Cross," Christine said and laughed. No one seemed to appreciate the joke.

Nick and Meg exchanged looks and followed Christine to the next habitat, which lit up as soon as they triggered the sensor. The landscaping inside the enclosure looked incomplete, like the installation crew had been interrupted halfway through and never came back to finish the job.

One side was a jungle setting with thick trunk trees with plenty of extended branches and tall grass. A ten-foot square section of flooring was covered with thick green mats that gymnasts might use for tumbling.

The other side of the large room was a playground with monkey bars, a dome-shape climbing structure, and hanging ropes. Three giant tractor tires were inside a large sandbox.

Four enormous chimpanzees that looked like they were pumped up on steroids were inside the enclosure. They loped about the habitat like a bunch of hairy bodybuilders eager to show off their stuff.

"These magnificent creatures are bili apes and are from the Democratic Republic of Congo."

"My God, they're the size of gorillas," Bob said.

"Some scientists believe they are a hybrid between chimp and gorilla." Christine said. "They're sometimes called the giant lion-eating chimp."

"I can believe it," Nick said, imagining these four slaughtering a lion. He'd heard news report stories about people being viciously attacked by pet chimpanzees and how they would go for soft spots of the body like the face and the genitals and brutally mutilate their prey.

"These particular bili apes are six feet tall, weigh close to 400 pounds, and are incredibly strong. Their muscle tissue is so dense, they're immune to both poison and tranquilizer darts."

"You make them sound unstoppable," Bob said.

"See those tractor tires? Each one of those weighs 1,500 pounds." Christine took a laser pen out of her pocket and shone the red beam through the glass. It only took a moment before a bili ape spotted the red dot on the floor and began following it over to one of the tractor tires. Christine shone the red dot inside the rubber housing.

The bili ape reached down, fit its fat fingers inside the rubber tread, and stood the huge tractor tire on end as though it was merely lifting a sheet of plywood that had fallen flat on the ground.

"Certainly wouldn't want one of those bad boys mad at me," Bob said.

"You can say that again," Nick agreed.

"Certainly wouldn't want—"

"Shut it," Nick said, cutting off his friend.

Nick watched a bili ape swing across the room on a rope and crash into the wall with such force it should have been knocked out cold. The big ape wasn't fazed in the least and scampered off like it was the funniest thing.

Another bili ape scampered up the metal framework of the monkey bars. It stood on the dome and roared, pounding its chest like King Kong standing on top of the Empire State Building. A smaller primate might have pulled it off as a cute display. Seeing the bili ape do it sent chills down Nick's spine. These were extremely dangerous animals.

"We have one more exhibit," Christine said.

"I don't think I'm going to be able to sleep tonight knowing these things are here," Meg said, as they walked behind the tour guide.

"Just think if they were to get out," Nick replied.

"Don't even kid around."

The next habitat had a jungle theme with a bamboo forest, large ferns, and dense broadleaf plants. Nick stared through the glass expecting to see something lurking behind the vegetation but saw nothing. "What are we looking for?" he finally asked.

"Somewhere behind those bushes is a Chinese wildman, the Asian version of our bigfoot, but much larger."

"How much bigger?" Bob asked.

"This creature stands about twelve feet tall and weighs over a thousand pounds."

"Holy shit, really?" Bob hadn't intended to swear and quickly apologized.

"And what's it called?" Nick asked.

"A yeren," Christine said.

"Wait a minute, I think I see something," Shane said.

Everyone watched as the plants parted and out stepped...

Professor Howard in her lab coat, taking a pleasant stroll through the jungle.

"Oh my God, what is she doing in there?" Meg asked.

Before Christine could answer, a giant ape stepped out of the brush and stood directly behind the woman. It was more than twice her height and had long orangey-brown hair over most of its body except for its black-skinned face and chest. It looked like an orangutan on growth hormones.

Some of the people were yelling and pounding on the glass to warn the professor.

She smiled back and waved.

The yeren reached down and placed a fur-covered hand on Professor Howard's shoulder. Its arm was as long as the woman was tall.

Professor Howard glanced up and patted the yeren's monstrous hand.

Nick grinned at Meg. "Jack Tremens better watch out. I think that big boy has a bit of a crush on the professor."

# 14

## ESCAPE ARTIST

The kraken clung to the coral reef and watched the fish swim by and disappear, only to reappear again in an endless parade. None of the occupants in the Tank paid any attention to the giant octopus camouflaged on the centerpiece of the aquarium and didn't consider it a threat as it kept to itself and normally preyed on crustaceans and mollusks.

But the eight-legged creature was becoming increasingly bored, its intelligent mind needing a challenge. It contemplated using its sharp beak to eat one of its arms for something to do as its primal urges compelled it to establish a more dominant role.

The underwater floodlights had been dimmed and the overhead lights on the other side of the glass were turned off in the observation room.

The octopus considered attacking a ten-foot long tiger shark gliding by. It would have to be extremely fast as the shark had exceptional vision in low-light conditions and would easily evade capture. Even if it was able to latch onto the shark, there was a great possibility that the other tiger sharks would think a feeding frenzy was taking place and gang up on the octopus.

That left the great white shark. Even though it was larger than the tiger sharks by an additional six feet, the octopus was confident that a one-on-one battle would be in its favor as long as the other sharks stayed out of the fray. Which meant timing the attack when the tiger sharks were on the opposite side of the reef.

The kraken moved slowly, its pigmentation reverting to its true self, as it climbed up the reef and pulled itself onto the other side.

It waited patiently as the tiger shark pack and a school of silvery fish passed by.

The great white came around the bend. It swam with a commanding presence as though it were the only animal in the aquarium. The white underbelly made the shark seem smaller and not as threatening but the kraken knew not to underestimate the carnivore as it was a vicious killer with massive jaws and flesh-ripping serrated teeth.

When the great white reached the midway point of the reef, the kraken thrust out its arms. Two appendages wrapped around the girth of the big fish. Each suction cup clamped down and fastened to the sandpapery skin of the shark, stopping it from swimming and preventing oxygen from passing through its gills.

Sensing that it was becoming oxygen deprived, the great white thrashed its body and tail in an attempt to break free.

Another of the kraken's arms shot out to wrap around the great white's head.

The great white bit off the arm with one savage bite.

Blue blood oozed out of the severed limb as it drifted down to the bottom of the aquarium, the tip of the appendage protruding out a few feet from behind the coral reef.

The kraken wrapped more of its arms around the great white, sealing the gills and muzzling the conical snout. The struggle was intense but brief. The giant octopus released its prey and the great white floated away just as the tiger sharks made their sweep around the reef, sensing a new source of food.

Not wanting to be mistaken as part of the meal, the giant octopus released a cloud of cephalopod ink, obscuring its retreat as it shot to the surface of the aquarium.

There was a one-foot gap between the water and the metal cover. The kraken saw the diver's hatch used for lowering the drums of krill. It grabbed the wheel on the hatch and turned it counter clockwise then pushed it up.

The opening was large enough for it to compress its arms and fit through, then drag its head out.

Once it was on the roof it quickly resumed its natural shape. Now that it was out of the water the only way it could survive was absorbing oxygen through its moist skin, but once it dried, the giant octopus would be unable to breathe and would quickly die.

Not wanting to return to the aquarium, it had to find another liquid habitat if it was to survive.

The octopus used its arms and scaled down the side of the building, breaking off a surveillance camera.

Ascending on a concrete walk, the octopod unfurled its arms and pulled itself sloppily along the ground toward a building with bright lights, and once there, emerged into the strange smelling water and hunkered down at the bottom.

# 15

## SKINNY DIPPING

Bob Pascale poured some scotch into his glass and took a gulp. He put the bottle on the small table by the sliding glass door. Rhonda had refused when he'd suggested they sit out on the enclosed patio and have drinks. He couldn't blame her, especially after the incident with the mothman.

Rhonda had propped herself up with some pillows on the bed and was watching an info commercial. A muscle bound hunk, glistening with sweat, was vigorously doing a strenuous workout on a multi-functional exercise machine.

"Maybe we should get one of those," Bob said, and flexed his bicep as he hoisted his glass to his lips.

"Why, our garage isn't cluttered enough?" Rhonda picked her glass up from the nightstand and took a swallow, dribbling some on the front of the white bathrobe provided by the hotel with the emblem WE above the breast pocket.

"You wouldn't like to see me buff like that?" Bob glanced at himself in the full-size mirror on the wall. He was wearing his Hawaiian shirt and matching swim shorts from their last vacation and a pair of brown flip-flops. His shirt was unbuttoned and open.

He often thought when he was younger that he looked a lot like Sean Connery in his James Bond days with his hairy chest and black hair. He still felt virile having the thick mat on his chest, as after sex, Rhonda would often lay beside him and pluck at it with her fingers.

The hair on his head had receded and thinned out.

He stared at his paunch straining his waistband.

Rhonda switched off the TV with the remote and swung her lithe legs off the side of the bed. "Let's go for a swim."

Bob checked his wristwatch. "It's after hours for the pool."

"So?"

"You want them to kick us out?"

"They're not going to do anything. What's the worst that could happen?" Rhonda said, slurring her words.

"I don't know," Bob said, hesitating, as he didn't know if he was really up for a night swim.

"Sure you won't change your mind?" Rhonda undid her sash and slowly opened the robe. She was completely naked underneath.

"Rhonda, you've had too much to drink."

"Not up for a little skinny dipping?" She patted barefoot across the carpet and grabbed the lapels of Bob's shirt. She stretched up on her tiptoes and planted a wet kiss on his lips. He could taste the alcohol on her hot breath. He knew there was no resisting her when she was in one of her sexy moods. Damn she looked good.

"All right. Better grab some towels," he said and went over to listen at the door connecting to the next suite. He couldn't hear the TV and figured the boys must have gone to bed.

Rhonda closed her bathrobe and slipped on a pair of sandals. She went into the bathroom and came out with two folded towels.

Bob made sure he had the keycard as they left the room. They went all the way down the hallway to the far elevator at the end of the corridor. Once they reached the ground floor, they'd be closest to the door leading out to the pool area and wouldn't have to worry about being noticed by anyone at the front desk as the lobby was around the corner.

As soon as the elevator doors opened, Bob and Rhonda snuck out quietly, went over to the door that led out to the pool, and crept outside.

Bob was relieved to see there were no other guests or employees around and that they had the Olympic-size pool all to themselves. The hotel lights shimmered on the surface of the chlorinated water. He walked over to the edge and looked down into the water but it was difficult to judge the depth with the black gunite on the bottom. It was like gazing down into a dark well.

He heard a splash and turned.

Rhonda popped her head out of the water. "What are you waiting for? Get in."

Bob watched as Rhonda dove and swam underwater, scissor-kicking her legs. He marveled at her tight buttocks as she passed by. She looked amazing, naked in the pool lights.

He was starting to get aroused.

Eager to get in the water, Bob began to take off his shirt just as Rhonda came to the surface. She stayed afloat and kept staring down in the water. "Bob? There's something moving on the bottom."

"Wait a second," he replied, kicking off his flip-flops and tossing his shirt on the nearest chaise lounge.

He turned around.

But Rhonda wasn't there.

He went to the edge of the pool and gazed into the water thinking she must have gone back under.

He couldn't see her anywhere so he walked along the edge.

"Rhonda?"

*This is weird, where'd she go?*

He looked over at the ladder thinking she had decided to climb out, but again, there was no sign of his wife.

"Rhonda, what the hell? Quit playing games."

*Had she drowned?*

He had to dive in and save her, but how, if he didn't know where she was?

"Honey, please...just tell me where—"

A gigantic arm burst out of the water and wrapped around Bob's bare chest and back, hoisting his feet off of the wet cement. He grabbed onto the slimy appendage hoping to pry himself loose but it was like being wrapped in the powerful coils of an enormous anaconda.

He quickly realized it wasn't a giant snake but the kraken.

*How the hell did it get out of the aquarium?*

It was crushing him like a vise.

Gasping for air, blood spurted out of his mouth. His ribcage splintered, puncturing his lungs and heart. He could feel the suction cups pulling the flesh from his body but not the pain associated with being skinned alive.

He quickly lost consciousness and was dragged down into the water to the bottom of the pool.

# 16

## DAMAGE CONTROL

Ivan Connors hadn't slept well since the park guests had arrived. As head of security it was his job to ensure everyone's safety and make sure none of Carter Wilde's bizarre menagerie of creatures killed anyone. He'd taken on dangerous assignments before, protecting Wilde Enterprises' expatriate employees in Third World countries from rebels and terrorists but that all seemed tame compared to overseeing the insane theme park.

He was constantly plagued by the adages *Expect the unexpected* and Murphy's law *Anything that can go wrong will go wrong* and felt like he was always one misstep away from treading on an inevitable landmine.

Ivan stood in the control room behind the chair of the security guard monitoring the flat screens covering one wall. He didn't envy the man's job, having to flit from screen to screen, systematically checking all forty for any suspicious activity.

"Is that the latest roster?" Ivan asked, glancing down at the man's desk.

"Yes, sir," the guard replied, never once taking his eyes off of the monitors as he handed Ivan the clipboard.

It was the complete list of everyone currently inside the dome. There was a tiny picture of each employee, copied from their ID badge and snapshots of family members so the security team could easily identify them.

He ran down the list to get a proper headcount:

SECURITY-18
MAINTENANCE AND GROUNDSKEEPERS-14
ZOOKEEPERS-10
HOTEL & RESTAURANT STAFF-17
TOUR GUIDES-3
LAB & WORKSHOP-11
BUS DRIVERS-2

PARK VISITORS-93
SPECIAL GUESTS-2

Ivan tabulated the numbers and came up with 170 people, counting himself, that he was responsible for. A daunting task, especially if something should go—

"Will you look at that?" exclaimed the guard seated at the desk.

"What is it?" Ivan said.

"Monitor 23."

Ivan placed his palms on the desk and leaned forward, catching a glimpse of a nude woman diving into the pool. A man was busily disrobing when the woman came to the surface. "Zoom in on her face."

The guard typed on his keyboard and a white box zoomed in and appeared around the woman's head. He enlarged the image.

Ivan glanced down the visitor list and got a photo match. "Rhonda Pascale." He looked up at the screen. "Let's hope the lucky schmuck is her husband."

The guard zoomed in on the man's face.

"Yep, that's Bob Pascale all right," Ivan said, confirming the image to the photograph on Pascale's badge ID.

"Wait a sec, where did she go?" The guard grabbed a joystick on his desk and began toggling the remote camera so they could get a wider sweep of the pool.

Rhonda Pascale had vanished.

Her husband was frantically pacing the edge of the pool.

"Holy shit!" the guard yelled when Bob Pascale was suddenly lifted off the ground.

"Oh my God!" Ivan said, feeling like he had just been kicked in the gut. "It's the damn kraken! How the hell did it get in the pool?"

The giant arm of the octopus slipped back in the water, taking the man with it.

"What do we do?" the guard asked, spinning around in his chair.

"I want a team over to the pool right away but no gunfire. I don't want to alarm the guests. Send another team over to the Tank. I need to make a quick call."

"Yes, sir."

Ivan retreated to his office and shut the door. The digital clock on his desk read 1:46 A.M. He didn't look forward to waking Carter Wilde so early in the morning but what choice did he have? Two people were dead.

He speed-dialed the number, put his cell phone to his ear, and waited for Carter Wilde to pick up. He answered on the fifth ring. "This better be important."

Ivan relayed the ghastly incident to his boss.

After almost a minute of dead air, Carter Wilde said, "Connors, I'm counting on you to resolve this problem."

"How so? Mr. and Mrs. Pascale are dead."

"I've known you to be resourceful."

"What, another cover up?" It was like the time Wilde had spun a story and told Ivan to send a team to eradicate a band of saboteurs that planned to blow up one of his refineries only to learn later that a small group of environmentalists had gone missing.

And now it was a Wilde Enterprises employee and his wife.

"I've invested too much time and money into this park. Don't screw this up."

"But sir."

"Get it done," Carter Wilde snapped and ended the call.

"Wilde, you son of a bitch." Ivan pocketed his phone, grabbed his two-way radio off the desk, and stormed out of his office.

"Is everyone in position?" Ivan asked, entering the control room.

"Yes, sir," replied the guard at the desk.

"Good. I'm going over to the pool. Tell the team at the Tank I'll be over there shortly."

"Should I call O'Brien?"

"No. I don't want her involved. Not just yet," Ivan said. There was no way he could cover up this mess if the marine biologist knew her main attraction had escaped and was killing guests.

He raced out of the security building and rushed over to the hotel. He cut through the rear downstairs hallway and went out the back to the pool.

Three of his men were standing at the edge of the pool and were staring down into the water. One of them spotted Ivan approaching and called out, "There's nothing down there."

"Keep your voice down," Ivan said. He joined the men and looked for himself.

All he could see was the black bottom of the pool.

"It must have crawled out. Spread out and canvas the area. I'm going over to the Tank."

The men fanned out and started their search.

Ivan double-timed over to the aquarium. The front entrance door was open and he went inside. Two of his men were waiting for him in the observation room.

"What do we have?" he asked.

One of the guards pointed through the glass.

Ivan could see the end of one of the octopus' arms extended beyond the edge of the reef. "Frigging thing's a regular Houdini."

"Roberts is up on the roof. He said you should come up."

Ivan walked through the building to the service elevator. He got in and rode it up to the roof. He stepped out and saw Roberts standing by the divers' station. Black wetsuits were hanging on the wall over a dozen oxygen tanks and other SCUBA equipment. A small crane with a swivel arm was mounted on the rooftop, next to 6 fifty-five gallon drums.

"It must have been a tight fit but I'm thinking it used this hatch." The guard stepped back to make room for his boss.

Ivan came over and looked at the upright hatch. The opening was maybe forty-eight inches across, large enough to pass down a large barrel, or in this case, big enough for a fifty-foot long octopus to squeeze through. "Close it up and put a lock on it."

"Yes, sir."

Satisfied that the culprit was contained, Ivan continued on with his plan and returned to the hotel. He'd brought along his most trusted man knowing he would be discreet and wouldn't ask any questions.

They went up to the Pascale's suite. Ivan used his master keycard, opened the door, and switched on the lights. The two entered and Ivan closed the door. He scanned the room then turned to the other man. "I want you to collect all of their belongings. Don't overlook anything."

"Yes, sir." The guard grabbed the two empty suitcases in the closet area across from the bathroom and threw them on the king-size bed. He went over to the dresser and yanked out each drawer, tossing bundles of clothes into the cases. He searched under the bed and picked up shoes and anything that had been left on the floor.

Ivan went into the bathroom. He picked up the small waste bin on the floor under the sink and began scooping combs, toothbrushes, cologne and other toiletry items off the counter into the plastic liner. Once the countertop was cleared off, he pulled the full bag out of the waste bin and placed it by the door leading out into the hall.

He came back into the suite and picked up the phone on the nightstand. "Front desk? I need for you to send someone up from housekeeping right away and give this place a thorough cleaning." He placed the receiver back on the cradle.

The guard finished packing everything up and put both cases on the floor. He pulled up the handles and dragged the wheeled luggage to the door. He took the suit bag off the clothes rod and draped it over one of the travel cases. "That's everything."

"You're sure?" Ivan asked.

"I even threw in the booze and their empty glasses."

"Good." Maybe this wasn't going to be as bad as he thought. Thanks to the kraken, at least he didn't have bodies to worry about. "Go ahead and put that in as well," Ivan said, pointing at the plastic bag by the door.

The guard unzipped a travel case, snatched the bag filled with toiletries and managed to flatten it inside with the clothes, then closed it up.

"What should I do with everything?" the guard asked.

"Take them to the furnace and burn them."

# 17

## THE REPTILE HOUSE

The next morning, Nick and Meg were about to leave their room to meet up with Bob, Rhonda, and the boys when there was a knock on the door.

Nick glanced at his wristwatch. "I wonder who that can be? We still have a few minutes."

"Maybe it's Gabe," Meg said, putting her purse strap over her shoulder.

The knocking persisted, this time a little louder.

"I'm coming," Nick said, crossing the room and opening the door. He was surprised to see a tall man dressed in a black security uniform.

"Nick Wells?" the man asked. He was holding a clipboard and had it tucked between his elbow and ribs.

"Yes."

"I'm Ivan Connors, in charge of security for the theme park. May I come in?"

"Ah, sure." Nick backed against the wall so Connors could enter the room.

Nick closed the door and followed Connors into the suite.

"Is everything all right?" Meg asked.

"I'm afraid I have some bad news, Mrs. Wells."

"Oh my God. Is it Gabe?" Meg put her hand up to her mouth.

"No, it's not your son. Bob Pascale had a massive heart attack."

"Is he okay?" Nick asked.

"I can't really say. We flew him out last night. His wife accompanied him."

"Does Shane know?"

"Not yet. That's why I'm here. I understand you and Mr. Pascale work in the same department."

"That's right."

"Are you and your families friends?"

"Yes, we are."

"Perhaps *you* could break the news to Shane. He might take it better if he heard it from someone he knew."

"I've a question. Why didn't they take Shane along?" Nick asked, thinking it was strange that Rhonda would leave her son behind.

"There wasn't enough room on the med-evac chopper."

"Oh. Sure, I'll talk to him," Nick said. He wasn't looking forward to telling the boy his father was seriously ill and had no idea how Shane would take it.

"Shane and our son, Gabe, are sharing a room," Meg said.

"I know. I have all that information right here on my roster," Connors said and showed them the clipboard. "I have to go. Again, I'm sorry." He turned to leave.

"You will keep us posted on Bob's condition?" Nick asked as he opened the door for Connors.

"As soon as I know something," Connors promised and walked out into the hall.

Nick closed the door and walked over to Meg.

"Oh my God, Nick."

"I'll admit, Bob wasn't in the best of shape and liked to drink, but I never thought he would have a heart attack. Hell, he's only thirty-seven."

"He's only a year older than you," Meg said. "So when do we tell Shane?"

"Right away. No point in putting it off," Nick said. "The longer we wait the harder it will be." He opened the door and they both went out.

A housekeeping cart was parked just down the hall next to an open door.

"That's Bob and Rhonda's room," Meg said.

Once they reached the cart, Nick stopped to glance inside the suite. A maid was wiping down the small table. The bed was made and everything looked in order.

"Where're Bob and Rhonda's stuff?" Meg asked. "I doubt they had time to pack."

"Someone must have collected their things."

"Who?"

Nick stepped in the doorway. "Excuse me?"

The maid stopped what she was doing and looked up. "Yes, sir?"

"The guests that were in this room. Where are their belongings?"

"I don't know, sir. I was told to clean the room."

Meg pulled on Nick's arm. "We can check with the front desk later."

"Okay." Nick waved at the maid. "Thank you."

They went to the next door and Nick knocked.

Gabe opened the door. "We're just about ready."

"We need to come in and speak with Shane," Nick said.

There were two twin beds in the suite. Nick and Meg sat on the edge of one bed while Shane sat on the other, so that they were facing each other. Gabe took a chair at the table.

Nick took a moment to collect his thoughts and said, "Shane, your father has suffered a heart attack. He's okay as far as we know but they had to airlift him to a medical facility. Your mom went as well."

Shane took it hard at first and began to cry. Meg jumped off the bed to sit beside him and put her arm around the boy's shoulder to console him, which helped to ease his pain as after a few more tears, he wiped his eyes and gave everyone a brave face. "Can we go have breakfast?"

"Sure, Shane."

The four of them left the room and went down to the dining area. Once again breakfast was served buffet-style. With everything going on, Nick had forgotten to bring along his binder so he couldn't do an on-the-spot evaluation of their meal, which was no better than the first day.

Once they were through eating, they went out by the pool area.

A sign was posted: POOL CLOSED UNTIL FURTHER NOTICE DUE TO MAINTENANCE.

"That sucks!" Gabe said.

"Yeah, big time," Shane chimed in.

Nick had to agree. So far, it seemed they were experiencing one letdown after another.

They joined up with the tour group and went on a short hike between the Bioengineering Laboratory and Animatronics Workshop Complex building and Sea Monster Cove to another spherical structure.

Christine led the way inside, which had the same floor plan as the Biped Habitat with a skylight and an observation room in the center.

"Welcome to The Reptile House," she said. "I'm sure many of you have heard the expression *when pigs fly.*"

Almost everyone nodded.

"Well, what about when snakes fly?"

"There's no such thing as a flying snake," a woman laughed.

"Oh, but there are. They are called arabhar and are from a region by the Arabian Sea. These snakes are aggressive and extremely venomous," Christine said and walked up to the dark pane glass, which suddenly became transparent as the lights lit up the enclosure on the other side of the divider.

The pie-shaped habitat looked like an oasis with a small pool surrounded by palm trees. Nick saw something that looked like a miniature parachute trick jumpers used, gliding across the water. Then he saw the snakehead and the tail. What he thought to be a parachute was actually four unfurled wings attached to the snake's ribcage enabling it to fly.

He could hear everyone's surprise, especially when three more snakes appeared out of the trees and took flight.

"That's totally crazy," Meg said to Nick.

"Kind of hard to top that."

But Nick was soon to be proven wrong when they stepped up to the next exhibit that lit up and had a Japanese theme with the facade of a house with paper walls. An area of sand had been raked flat and was next to a water garden with a small footbridge spanning a pond filled with a dozen large orange and white carp. Nick saw what he initially thought was a tire, appear from behind the paper house and roll out onto the sand. When it came to a stop, Nick quickly realized that it was a fat snake with its tail in its mouth, taking on the shape of a wheel.

"Well, I guess that's a bit faster than crawling," he quipped.

"That is a tzuchinoko," Christine said. "They are quite unique. There are actually two in this exhibit." She took a few seconds to look for the other one. "Oh, there it is."

Nick saw the other snake. Instead of slithering on the ground, it was able to leap, covering three-foot stretches at a time. It looked to be about five feet long and was so thick he wouldn't have been surprised if it weighed 100 pounds. It had a thin tail at the end of its fat body.

"Again, these Japanese snakes are very dangerous," Christine said, not that anyone was going to doubt her word, especially when one of the snakes came up to the glass, opened its giant mouth and hissed, exposing four-inch long fangs.

"Not so friendly, is it?" Meg said.

"Hey, check these guys out," Shane shouted.

Nick saw that Shane and Gabe had gotten ahead of the tour group. Normally, he would have told the boys to get back with the others but he didn't want to sound like he was scolding them, figuring Shane was going through enough and didn't need any added stress.

Three giant lizards roamed the next enclosure landscaped with dirt and knee-high grass, strewn boulders, and a 10 by 20 foot in-ground Fiberglas swimming pool. They were fifteen feet long with bony-ridged backs and powerful tails. Each foot on their stumpy short legs had eight-inch long claws.

"These monitor lizards are called Buru and are from India."

A Buru standing in the grass let out a hoarse bellow.

"Just like a komodo dragon," Christine said, "a Buru has so much bacteria in its mouth, a single bite will cause the victim's body to rot."

"Talk about dragon breath,' Meg said.

Nick noticed that Shane and Gabe had split away from the group, again, and were already to the next exhibit. "Come on," he said to Meg. "We have to keep moving."

Christine saw the teenagers and hurried everyone along.

The overhead lights on the other side of the glass came on. The landscape was rolling dunes like in the Sahara Desert.

"Here we have Mongolian death worms," Christine announced. "Found only in the Gobi Desert."

"I don't see anything," a man said, disappointedly.

"That's because they live in the sand and burrow underground."

"So how do we see them?" asked the same man.

"Easy." Christine went up to a push-button pad on the wall. She tapped a key.

Water shot out of an overhead sprinkler and rained down on a section of sand. A few seconds later, an enormous hideous-looking worm punched out of the wet sand. It curled up, raised its eyeless head, and opened its round mouth, revealing a ring of sharp, pointy teeth.

"These twenty-foot-long creatures have the ability to shock their prey and are attracted to sound," Christine said and pushed another button on the pad.

A speaker mounted on a pole in the sand began to make a thrumming noise.

The sound was enough to draw another worm out of the sand. It turned its sightless head and faced everyone staring from the other side of the glass, sensing the vibration of shuffling feet.

A thick salivary goop shot out of the worm's mouth and splattered the window.

"That icky stuff is venom," Christine said.

"Jesus, Nick," Meg said. "That thing must be twenty feet away."

"What if you were to touch one?" Nick asked.

"I'm afraid you'd die. Well, that concludes our tour of The Reptile House," Christine said and signaled for everyone to follow her out.

"House of Horrors, you mean," Nick muttered to Meg as they funneled down the hall with the others toward the nearest exit door.

# 18

## THE CHILDREN

Jack and Miguel were just finishing up with lunch.

The buffet was Italian cuisine with abundant helpings of sliced pizza, spaghetti and meatballs, baskets of garlic bread, eggplant Parmesan, lasagna, ricotta and meat cannelloni, cheese-stuffed tortellini, fettuccine, and other pastas.

There were even pony-sized bottles of assorted wines for the adults.

Miguel preferred Mexican food but had no problem wolfing down three slices of pepperoni pizza and polishing off two bottles of red wine.

Jack took the last bite of his eggplant Parmesan, put his fork down, and pushed himself away from the table. "Man, am I stuffed."

"You're getting spoiled," Miguel said, sitting back in his chair and crossing his arms.

"And you're not? I don't hear you complaining." Jack knew Miguel often bragged he would rather rough it in the outdoors than stay in some fancy hotel. But lately it seemed Miguel wasn't so anxious to jump at their next assignment as he once was. Jack suspected that his friend missed his family and wanted to go home to spend time with them, which wouldn't be long as they would no longer be contractually obligated to Carter Wilde once the theme park opened.

Now it was just a matter of hanging around and hoping they didn't die of boredom.

"Thought I might pay Nora a visit," Jack said. "Care to come along?"

"And cramp your style?"

"Like you could do that. Come on, you could use the exercise."

Jack and Miguel got up from the table, bussed their trays over to the trash bin, and went outside. They followed the pathway to the Bioengineering Lab and entered the building. Jack used his access card and opened the door to the laboratory.

Nora was standing next to a wire cage, watching the pregnant chupacabra, its belly fully extended, lapping up blood from a small pan.

"Hey," Jack greeted. "She looks about ready to burst."

"Won't be long," Nora said, beaming as if she were a close relative to the expecting mother instead of a scientist waiting for an abomination to deliver.

Jack noticed a movie camera on the counter. "Are you planning to film the birth?"

"Yes, unless one of you would like to assist?" Nora asked.

"I was in the delivery room when Maria had Sophia," Miguel said.

"So you want to do it?"

"Not really, but for you I will."

"Thanks, Miguel. Would you both like to come back and see the children?"

"Sure," Jack said. He glanced around and was glad to see that Dr. McCabe was not around. There was something about the man that made Jack feel uneasy. He never liked the idea of Nora working in the same room with the man.

Nora led the way through the laboratory to a door in the back. She slid a keycard in the reader and the door swished open.

Jack and Miguel followed Nora into the nursery where they were assaulted by a barrage of chattering, chirping, and strange devilish cries.

The room sounded like the inside of a pet store.

There were different sized cages and glass enclosures against the wall to accommodate the occupants depending on their stages of development.

Jack saw thunderbird and kongamatok chicks perched in wire cages. Across the aisle were small habitats with baby bigfoot and white yetis. In a playpen were a couple of sauropods that looked like plastic figurines until they moved in their slow fashion. A blue tiger cub was fast asleep in a cage. Inside a tall enclosure stood a four-foot tall six-month-old yeren.

He spotted more innocent-looking cryptid infants lazing about, too young to be of any real threat but in time would become too dangerous to handle.

"How would you two like to help with the bottle-feeding?" Nora asked.

"Okay by me," Jack said. He looked at Miguel.

"Sure, why not. It's not like there's anything else around here for us to do."

# 19

## MAMMOTH ARENA

The round concrete structure looked like an enormous fort, stretching up more than a hundred feet. Of all the exhibit buildings, this was the largest and was at the rear of the dome.

Nick leaned back to look up. "Kind of reminds me of that wall in the King Kong movie the natives built to keep out the big ape."

"Please don't tell me that's what's inside," Meg said.

"Hey, in this place nothing would surprise me." Which wasn't exactly true. Ever since they had arrived, everything had surprised him. Even though he had his reservations about the theme park and questioned if it was really a safe place for families to visit, he had to admit it sure had its appeal and billions of people from all over the world would flock to see it.

Cryptid Zoo had the potential of becoming the number one attraction on the planet. The only things missing were amusement rides and concession stands which could be integrated as afterthoughts seeing as there was ample space on the grounds between the existing buildings: suggestions that Nick planned to include on his evaluation sheet.

Christine stood facing the group at the front entrance of the building and said, "Welcome to Mammoth Arena. Even though you have seen some amazing creatures on our other tours, I would like to think we left the best for last. If everyone—"

A horrendous roar bellowed from within the steep-wall enclosure.

"Oh my God," Meg said.

"What the hell was that?" a woman asked nervously, grabbing onto her husband.

"You'll soon see," Christine replied, unflinchingly. "Now, if everyone will please come this way."

As they entered, Nick caught a strong whiff of feces and smells associated with large animals. He looked up. He could see the I-beam girders high up inside the dome, as there was no ceiling on the building.

Two enclosures, a combination of wire-cage and glass took up a portion of the ground floor, flanked by a high wall where a steel spiral staircase wormed up to the top.

"Mommy, look," a little girl yelled excitedly, "Blue tigers."

Two huge tigers with blue fur were lying on a platform behind the thick glass of the observation window.

"That's right," Christine said. "Maltese tigers actually, from the Fujian Province of China."

"Big deal. So you dyed them," Shane said.

Even though Shane could be a pain in the ass, Nick was glad to see that he was in true form and no longer seemed upset about his father.

"No, they weren't dyed. One has the allele gene, which has the unusual trait to cause an abnormality in the pigmentation; in this case, the color blue. The other tiger is a clone and is an exact replica, right down to each hair fiber."

Nick had to admit they looked identical. It was like one tiger was lying next to a mirror image of itself. "How much do they weigh?" he asked.

"They each weigh exactly the same: nine hundred and sixty-three pounds. That makes them the second largest big cats in the world."

"Holy cow," a woman said.

"If you think they're impressive, take a look at our mngwa, which is Tanzanian for 'giant cat.'" Christine said. She stepped away from the tigers and directed everyone's attention to the other enclosure.

Nick remembered when they had first entered the dome and saw the plaque on the pedestal of the covered statue that had the same name, though at the time he had no idea what it meant.

Two black panthers were pacing inside the glass enclosure. Each one was as tall as a mule.

"These look bigger than the tigers," Nick said.

"That's right," Christine confirmed. "These bioengineered animals are male and female and we hope will become a mated pair. The male is slightly larger and weighs just under twelve hundred pounds, the female, a thousand."

"Making them the largest in the cat family," Nick concluded.

"Exactly," Christine said. "Now, if you will all follow me, we have a bit of a climb ahead of us." She walked over to the bottom step of the spiral staircase and began to go up.

Nick counted one hundred seventy-seven steps by the time they reached a catwalk that ran along the top of the wall encompassing a circular area half the size of a football field above two separate open-air habitats.

"Please hold onto your children's hands and no hanging over the railing," Christine instructed. "As you can see, it's quite a drop to the bottom."

"Oh my God, Nick. Look at the size of that thing!" Meg said.

"Jesus, is that a bear?"

Christine must have heard Nick because she then said, "That's right. You are looking at Bergman's bear, named after the Swedish zoologist Sten Berman who claimed to have tracked one down in Russia. This particular animal stands sixteen feet tall and weighs over four thousand pounds."

Nick had seen pictures of adult grizzlies and polar bears and thought they were huge but Bergman's bear put them all to shame and made them look like cubs in comparison. He could feel the platform vibrate as it lumbered about its enclosure. It stood on its hind legs and scratched its back against the concrete wall, brushing off small pieces of cement. He wondered if there was any threat of the wall crumbling. Surely someone was monitoring the bear's activity. He'd have to make a special note in his report.

The bear gazed up and saw everyone staring down. It opened its maw and let out a thunderous roar, the same sound they had heard earlier.

Even from where he stood, almost seventy feet above the bear, Nick swore he could feel the heat of its breath on his face.

He turned and saw that some of the group were already following Christine as she walked around the observation deck toward the other habitat, which was overgrown with fifty-foot tall eucalyptus trees, high grass, and yuccas.

Christine waited until everyone was situated before saying, "Here we have the giant ground sloth, also called Megatherium."

It took a second or two before Nick saw the mammoth creature through the tree branches. It was bigger than Bergman's bear and much stockier. A five-foot long tongue wrapped around a low-hanging branch and stripped off the leaves.

"This creature is believed to have lived in the Early Pliocene period. It weighs a whopping four tons and stands over twenty feet tall. As you can see, it has massive claws. They are so long that it can't put its soles flat on the ground and must walk on the sides of its feet."

"Those claws look like they could do some serious damage," Meg said.

Nick had to agree. Each claw was curved and had to be at least two feet long.

"Some paleontologists believe the ground sloth was carnivorous and may have even hunted saber-toothed tigers."

"Yeah, right," Shane said disbelievingly.

Carnivorous or not, Nick couldn't help worrying what kept the gargantuan creature from digging its way out or clawing through the cement, thoughts that continued to nag him even after the tour ended and they'd left the building.

# 20

## FEEDING TIME

Tilly O'Brien sat in the driver's seat of the Cushman while Cam Morgan lifted another bin of freshly butchered meat onto the flatbed. He pushed the container up against the other food bins then came around and scooted onto the front passenger seat.

"We're good to go," Cam said.

Tilly pressed down on the accelerator and the electric cart took off, humming down the long tunnel at 5 miles an hour.

The beams of the small headlights were only good for a short distance, which was adequate whenever they were in the vicinity of the yellow globe lights staggered throughout the tunnels, though some places were pitch black in the dark maze.

Another Cushman exited an adjacent tunnel and came right at them, the driver blinding them with a powerful spotlight, forcing Cam and Tilly to shield their eyes.

Tilly swerved and almost crashed against the sidewall.

"Beecher, knock off the shit or I'm going to kick your ass!" Cam yelled at the man in the other vehicle as it narrowly missed them as it went by.

"Got to catch me first!"

Cam turned in his seat to issue another tirade but Beecher had already vanished down the tunnel.

"One of these days his pranks are going to get someone hurt," Tilly said.

"Killed is more like it. Hopefully one day he'll be the brunt of his own joke. Who are we feeding first?"

"The bipeds," Tilly said.

"Shouldn't we be bringing a goat for the chupacabras?"

"Dr. McCabe sent me an e-mail asking that we don't feed them tonight."

"I don't think he likes the little bloodsuckers much," Cam said. "I've seen the way he treats them. There's something about that guy."

"Yeah, I know what you mean. I've never really liked him." Tilly pulled into a small parking area and turned off the Cushman.

Cam climbed out and walked around to the back while Tilly grabbed the pushcart parked by the wall and brought it over.

They dragged eight bins off the flatbed and stacked them on the cart.

Cam pushed the loaded cart over to the elevator marked: BIPED HABITAT EMPLOYEES ONLY. He tapped the up button and the doors opened. They got inside and rode up to the main floor.

When the elevator stopped, they stepped out into a curved corridor that ran around the back walls of each habitat.

"You know it'd go faster if we split up," Cam said. Standard procedure dictated that two zookeepers worked together at all times during feeding times to ensure each one's safety.

"You know the rules," Tilly said.

"Let's start with the yeren and work our way around then."

"Okay."

Cam pushed the cart down the corridor and stopped at the first door.

He grabbed the keycard hanging from a lanyard around his neck and swiped the reader on the wall. The lock disengaged and he opened the door. An overhead light automatically came on in a small room slightly bigger than a broom closet.

Tilly stepped inside first and flipped on a few breakers, turning on four flat screen monitors on the wall. Each image on the screens was a different angle of the yeren's jungle enclosure.

The giant ape-like creature was nowhere to be seen.

"I have to say for being such a big guy, he sure knows how to make himself scarce," Cam said, carrying in a bin full of bunched bananas and guava fruit.

"Are you set?" Tilly asked.

"Open it," Cam replied.

Tilly ran her keycard down the lock release and pushed the door open.

Cam immediately stepped through the doorway and spilled the mixed fruit onto the ground. He wasn't too worried, as the yeren never exhibited any violent behavior and was more of a gentle giant.

But his training taught him never to take chances so he stepped quickly back into the room. Tilly immediately closed the door and set the lock.

They moved on to the bigfoot habitat. One monitor showed a bigfoot halfway across the enclosure, sleeping on a pile of pine needles.

The image of the second bigfoot was on another screen, sitting by the berry bush.

"What do you think?" Tilly asked.

"This might be a good time," Cam said, figuring the bigfoot squatting on the ground was probably twenty feet away from the door, giving him more than enough time to open the door and throw out some meat and fruit before it tried to rush at him.

As soon as Tilly opened the door, Cam took a single step out and tossed the shanks of meat and raw fruit out onto the ground. He stepped back and Tilly shut the door.

They proceeded to the yeti habitat.

Cam stood by the door with a container of meat. "You know, at first I had trouble telling them apart."

"Not anymore," Tilly said.

Cam looked up at the monitors. He saw the pristine-white yeti sitting in the fake snow—Burt Owen's animatronic.

The other yeti—the bioengineered one—was standing at the mouth of the cave with bloodstains on its fur.

"Ready?" Tilly asked.

"Go!"

Tilly opened the door wide enough so Cam could chuck out the meat then slammed it closed.

They left the room and proceeded down the corridor, bypassing the chupacabras' habitat and stopping at the bili apes' enclosure.

Cam grabbed a bin off the pushcart. Tilly held the door for him as he stepped inside the staging room.

Tilly turned on the monitors.

The four apes were sitting on the tractor tires, facing each other, like a congregation of conspiring thugs.

Tilly looked at Cam. "You want to come back, maybe then they'll be asleep?"

"No, let's just get this over with." Cam knew Tilly dreaded whenever they had to feed the massive apes, as they were unpredictable brutes, which was why none of the other zookeepers would get near the creatures.

"In and out." Tilly poised herself by the door. "Ready?"

"Go!"

Tilly slid her keycard and swung the door open.

Cam stepped out with the bin of meat and slipped on a slimy puddle of urine. He fell back against the door causing it to slam shut.

He immediately scrambled to his feet, his hands and clothes reeking of primate piss. He shot a glance over at the tractor tires.

The bili apes were gone.

"Shit!" Cam turned and slammed his fist on the door. "Tilly! Open the damn door."

He could hear the bili apes stampeding toward him.

The door remained closed.

"Damn it, Tilly." He glanced over his shoulder.

The muscular apes charged through the fake jungle setting, howling and baring their teeth like a bunch of lunatic escapees from an insane asylum.

In seconds they would be upon him, grabbing his arms and legs, ripping them clear out of the sockets, disemboweling him with their bare hands as they chewed off his face and ate his penis and ripped off his balls.

Suddenly, the door opened and Cam dove into the room onto the floor.

Tilly pulled the door closed.

The apes crashed into the barrier. Cam thought for sure the door was going to come off its hinges but it was thick-gauged steel and held. The monstrous primates screeched and slammed their fists on the door and surrounding wall.

Tilly dropped to her knees and looked at Cam. "Thank God you're okay."

"Jesus, Tilly, didn't you hear me calling you?"

"I couldn't open the door."

"What do you mean?"

"There was some kind of malfunction. My keycard wouldn't work. I had to override the lock with the emergency release."

"Shit, that's not good."

# 21

## BIG MISTAKE

Gabe had become sleepy watching TV and had just dozed off when Shane plopped on the side of his bed and startled him awake.

"Get up, Gabe. We're going out!"

Gabe sat up and gazed about the room. "What time is it?"

"Hell, I don't know," Shane said, jumping up and pacing the floor. "Let's go and explore."

Gabe glanced over at the clock radio on the nightstand. "Shane, it's two in the morning."

"So?"

"I don't think they want us roaming around out there without supervision."

"What, now you're a kindergartener?" Shane took a moment and gave Gabe the royal stare down. "Or maybe you're chicken? Need to get mommy's permission?"

"Shut up, and stop being a jerk!" Gabe didn't like it when Shane made wisecracks about his parents, especially his mom. Even though he was always going over and hanging out with Shane, Gabe never considered him a close friend, as he was too bossy and obnoxious. It was just an excuse to get out of the house.

"Fine, stay, you little pansy." Shane put on his sweatshirt, pulled the hood up over his head, and started for the door.

Gabe was feeling wide-awake after their little altercation and knew there was no way he was going sleep. Maybe it would be fun sneaking out, just as long as they didn't get caught. "Okay, I'm coming."

"Well, will you looky here. Gabe just found his balls."

"Yeah, and you're still an ass."

"Touché brother."

Gabe put on his hooded sweatshirt too; that way he could keep his face from being seen by any surveillance cameras. He'd seen a few of the security guards walking the premises, some of them looking tough enough to maybe have been cops or servicemen in the military.

The last thing he wanted was to embarrass his dad in front of his work buddies, but then he figured the worst that could happen was they'd get a warning and be escorted back to the hotel.

No harm, no foul.

They snuck out of their room and tiptoed down the hallway.

"We'll take the stairs," Shane said.

Gabe followed Shane to the fire door. They quietly entered the stairwell and crept down the cement steps all the way to the ground floor.

"What if there's an alarm?" Gabe asked, as Shane put both hands on the push bar on the exit door.

"Only one way to find out." Shane shoved the door open.

No alarm sounded; at least, none that they could hear.

When they stepped outside it was dark and Gabe expected to see a night sky full of stars. Instead, he saw the massive underbelly structure of the dome roof looming 25 stories above their heads.

They cut around the backside of the hotel.

Gabe noticed a sign that the pool was closed. He could hear weird birdcalls coming from the Aviary. Bergman's bear's bestial roar boomed from the far side of the cavernous stadium.

The grounds reminded Gabe of pictures he'd seen of Central Park in the evening as they kept to the shadows to avoid being spotted by anyone out patrolling the premises.

There were lampposts illuminating the pathways and decorative outdoor lighting positioned around the plants and shrubs surrounding the nearby buildings.

"Where are we going?" Gabe whispered, scurrying after Shane.

"You'll see. Come on!" Shane dashed off and Gabe followed closely behind as they bolted down the walkway and sprinted up the hill.

"What are we doing here?" Gabe asked when they passed by the Sea Monster Cove sign.

"I'm going to prove to you the sea serpent is fake. A million dollars it's one of Burt Owen's animatronics."

"Like you got a million dollars."

"You know what I mean," Shane said, strutting off.

Gabe followed him over to the bleachers and they quietly stepped down each row until they reached concrete steps that stretched almost to the water's edge. The surface was inky black except for a luminous shimmer from a single light on the bank. A sleepless sauropod let out a *wonk* inside the cave.

Water slopped up against the concrete wall.

"It's swimming around down there," Gabe said, watching the water ripple.

"Probably just some pumps," Shane scoffed.

"You saw it when it jumped out of the water," Gabe said, thinking back when they had witnessed the cadborosaurus leap out of the cove to catch the fish Christine had released down the chute. "Tell me that wasn't real?"

"Hey, I'm telling you it's a mechanical sea serpent on a track like the *Jaws* shark that attacks that ride at Universal Studios. Let's get closer and I'll prove it."

"You really think that's a good idea?"

But before Shane could answer, the sea monster's head burst out of the water like an exploding geyser, drenching Gabe and Shane. It raised its long neck and stared down at the two teenagers.

"Run!" Shane screamed.

Gabe scrambled right behind Shane.

The sea serpent let out a strange bellow and lunged across the water, its mouth gaping open. It snapped its teeth, narrowly missing Gabe as he scampered up the concrete steps. He was too scared to look back.

They reached the lower row of the bleachers and kept climbing.

Gabe heard a loud splash. He turned around and saw that the sea serpent had submerged. "Think it's fake now?" he yelled at Shane as they made it to the platform.

"Big deal, so it's real," Shane said, stopping to catch his breath.

No matter what, Gabe knew Shane would always find a way of spinning things around so he wouldn't look stupid.

Gabe saw a big glob of gelatin dragging itself over the platform.

"Hey, will you looky there?" Shane said. "If it ain't the globster. Now *that* I know is fake for sure."

Gabe watched the organic blob reach out with its tiny arms and pull itself slowly toward them. Up close it looked like a big tadpole with black-globed eyes and an oval-shaped mouth. Gabe almost felt sorry for it.

"There's no way that thing's real," Shane said. He glanced around and spotted a gaff leaning against the wall. He grabbed the pole, walked up to the globster, and drove the barbed spear deep inside the bizarre creature.

The globster didn't even flinch.

"See, I told you," Shane said. He pulled out the gaff. The tip of the shaft was dripping with a jelly-like slime. He tossed the pole on the platform.

"Better watch out," Gabe warned. Tendrils of acrid smoke were rising from the metal spearhead and wooden shaft.

"What, you think it's going to eat me or something?" Shane squatted and waved his hand in front of the globster's face to taunt it. He looked over at Gabe. "See, there's nothing—"

The globster took Shane's arm into its mouth.

"Holy shit," Shane screamed.

Gabe didn't know what to do. He certainly didn't want to get too close but then he knew he had to help. Shane struggled but the globster refused to open its mouth. "Help me, Gabe. Don't just stand there. Do something."

But what could he do? There was no way he was going to touch that thing. Could it really be a washed-ashore carcass? And if so, it had to be crawling with bacteria and pathogens, for sure that flesh-eating disease.

Gabe rushed over anyway and grabbed Shane around the waist. "On the count of three try and pull out your arm." Gabe planted his feet to push off. "One...two...THREE!"

They fell back and landed on the platform.

Gabe scrambled to his feet.

The globster gazed up with a blank expression.

Shane looked at his freed arm and screamed.

Gabe glanced down and saw that the sleeve of Shane's sweatshirt had been dissolved away into holey tatters, revealing a shriveled, oozing appendage with webbed nubs for fingers on a wilted hand.

It wasn't until he saw the flesh bubbling on Shane's grotesque shrunken arm that he threw up on his sneakers.

# 22

## CAVE-IN

Tilly could tell Cam was still a little shaken up after the incident with the bili apes as they stepped out of the elevator onto the parking area. "Hey, if you want I can drop you off and I'll finish up?"

"No, I'm fine."

"You sure?"

"Yeah. I'm not afraid to admit I was scared shitless back there."

"You and me both."

"We need to file a report."

"I agree and we will," Tilly said. "Want to drive?" She figured it might take Cam's mind off nearly getting killed. At least he wasn't shaking like he'd been coming down the elevator.

"All right." He got behind the wheel and Tilly slid onto the passenger seat.

Cam swung the electric cart around and headed down the tunnel.

They were following the passage to the next enclosure when they saw a maintenance man in an orange and yellow vest, standing by the main electrical junction box station that controlled the power network for the entire dome.

"Pull over," Tilly said. "Let's tell him about the faulty door at the bili ape habitat and he can relay a message to have someone check it out."

Cam slowed down and stopped.

The worker had his back turned and was in front of a large control panel with the doors standing wide open.

"Excuse me," Tilly called out.

The man ignored her and kept on working intently under the light of his helmet lamp. A workbag with orange and yellow stripes was by his feet.

"Hey, buddy!" Cam yelled, but again, the man didn't respond.

"Maybe he's wearing earbuds," Tilly said.

"Or he's hard of hearing. Let's go, we can report it later." Cam tramped on the accelerator and the Cushman hummed down the passage.

They were heading down the tunnel that led under Mammoth Arena when Cam suddenly slammed on the brakes. "Jesus, will you look at that?" Cam slid out from behind the steering wheel and stood next to the electric cart.

He walked up to the large chunk of concrete in the middle of the passageway that was as big as a crumpled refrigerator.

Tilly looked up and saw a similar sized hole in the ceiling.

"What do you think caused that?" Cam asked.

As if answering his own question, they felt the ground tremble and heard a rumble from above.

"It's the bear and the sloth," Tilly said. "They should never have run a tunnel under that enclosure." She'd voiced her concern to deaf ears that the behemoth creatures were much too heavy and might cause seismic damage but of course no one listened, and now there was the proof, staring her right in the face. "Go around."

Cam got back behind the wheel, tromped on the accelerator, and steered around the obstruction.

"Turn left at the next bend for the Reptile House." Tilly held onto the side railing as Cam cut the sharp turn. Again, he had to stomp on the brakes.

A Mongolian death worm appeared from behind a six-foot tall squatty pyramid of sand in the center of the roadway. It manipulated the bristles on its segmented body and pulled itself across the asphalt.

Tilly looked up and saw a gaping hole, the size of a large manhole in the ceiling. Another giant worm slipped down out of the orifice and landed on the mound of sand.

"Cam, we need to get out of here. Now!"

"Jesus!" Cam cranked the steering wheel and put the cart into reverse to turn around. The back of the vehicle slammed against the curved wall with a crunch. He spun the wheel and the vehicle crept down the tunnel as the speed governor on the cart wouldn't allow them to go any faster than 5 miles an hour.

Tilly glanced over her shoulder.

All four of the humongous worms had escaped their containment and were slithering down the tunnel, drawn to the sound of the Cushman's spinning tires and the electrical hum of its motor.

An earthshaking explosion sounded down the passage.

"What the hell was that?" Cam yelled out.

But before Tilly could answer, a billowing cloud of dust appeared out of the tunnel and swept over them.

# 23

## BREECH

Ivan had been sleeping in his office when he felt the couch beneath him shake and heard the lamp on his desk topple off the edge and crash onto the floor. He sat up just as the door flung open and the security guard on duty stepped into the doorway.

"What just happened?" he asked, noticing that his office was bathed with a yellowish glow from the emergency lights out in the hall.

"There's been an explosion."

"Where?"

"I'm not sure but the entire electrical grid is down. There's no surveillance cameras, computers, nothing."

"I want everyone in the armory," Ivan said, grabbing his boots and putting them on. "No one leaves the hotel. Alert the zookeepers."

"What should I tell them?"

"Tell them we have a serious problem. Without electricity, all the actuators in the electronic door locks are going to deactivate."

The guard gave him a blank expression.

"Means those doors in the animal enclosures are no longer locked."

\*\*\*

Nick woke up when he heard what sounded like an air raid siren. He got up out of bed and rushed to the window. It was too dark to see anything, as there were no lights on around the pool area or anywhere else for that matter.

"What is that godawful noise?" Meg grumbled and sat up in bed.

"I don't know. It looks like the entire dome has gone dark. Maybe we had an earthquake. I thought I felt something earlier but figured it was you rolling over in bed."

"Very funny."

"No, really." Nick grabbed his jeans and a T-shirt off the back of the chair by the small table.

"What are you doing?" Meg asked.

"Going outside to see what's going on."

"Hold on, I'm going with you."

They hustled and got dressed.

"We better check on the boys and make sure they're okay," Nick said, opening the door leading out into the hall. He noticed a man standing in his doorway, wearing only a pair of boxers. Yellow emergency lights lit up portions of the hall.

"Any idea what's going on?" the man asked.

"Not really. Looks like the power went out," Nick told him.

The man closed the door.

Nick and Meg hurried down the hall. He knocked on the door to the boys' room.

After a few seconds, he knocked again.

"Surely, they can't be sleeping through all that racket," Meg said.

"Gabe, open the door!" Nick pounded on the door some more.

"You don't think they snuck out, do you?" Meg asked.

"Better not or they're—"

The door opened slightly and Gabe peered out.

"There's something going on outside," Nick said. "We need you both to come with us."

"Shane's not feeling so well."

"All right, he can stay. Grab your clothes."

Gabe shut the door and less than a minute later came out of the room and closed the door behind him.

"Let's go down to the lobby," Nick said. "Maybe the desk clerk can tell us what's going on." They made their way down to the end of the hallway. Nick wasn't surprised when he saw the elevator button on the wall wasn't lit up. "Looks like we're taking the stairs."

\*\*\*

The bili apes screeched when their habitat suddenly went dark before the emergency lights came on. One of the primates threw itself up against the glass door as it had done many times before, only this time the door swung open. The ape tumbled out, executed a tight-rolled somersault, and landed on its feet. It gazed around, unsure of its newfound freedom.

The burly primate let out a loud shriek, which brought the other three apes running. They gathered in the middle of the observation area and formed a tight revolving circle, backs pressed against each other in a defensive stance as they gradually became aware of the other creatures staring at them from the other gloomy habitats.

The bili apes separated and began to strut about, grunting and huffing, exhibiting aggressive behavior and slapping their chests, ready to take on any adversary.

The yeren watched with disinterest as they passed by.

Both of the bigfoots stood a few feet behind the threshold of their ajar door. Even though they were outnumbered two to one, they showed no fear.

The bioengineered yeti glared at the massive apes and even snarled as they ambled past while the animatronic yeti merely watched, sitting by the cave.

Knowing when best to run and hide, the frightened chupacabras slunk back into the shadows of their habitat.

The bili apes screeched, and with a burst of energy, barreled down the corridor toward the front entrance and smashed their way out of the building.

\*\*\*

The ground shook and a fissure opened up under the foundation of the high wall surrounding Mammoth Arena. Gray dust rose in the air. A zigzagging crack rippled up the concrete causing chunks to break away and fall out. A section of wall collapsed into rubble leaving a massive gaping hole.

Bergman's bear saw an opportunity to escape. It lumbered on all fours across the enclosure and was about to climb out over the fallen debris when it was met by the giant ground sloth blocking its way. The enormous bear rose up on its hind legs and roared.

The blue tigers paced their habitat, sensing that something wasn't right when they heard the commotion on the other side of the enclosure. They noticed the glass door was wide open and slipped out. The tigers paraded down the hall, side by side like two identical bookends.

The two mngwas watched the tigers stride out of the building then stealthily crept out of their habitat. They were extremely hungry having not eaten. The giant leopards bounded down the corridor in search of food.

\*\*\*

It didn't take long for the three giant monitor lizards to escape. The Burus stuck out their serpentine tongues in hopes of picking up a scent as they did a belly run on their short legs, wiping their crocodilian bodies forward with their powerful tails.

An arabhar flew out of the Reptile House to catch up with the other three flying snakes that had already managed to flee the building.

The two tzuchinoko snakes decided on an easier route made by the Mongolian death worms. The fat Japanese snakes slithered down through the sand into the tunnel below.

\*\*\*

The claxton pointed in the direction of the Aviary continued to blare from the mast mounted on the roof of the hotel. The piercing wail was more than the thunderbirds could endure. Shrieking, the enormous birds attacked the steel netting with their giant beaks, ripping sizeable holes. They held on with their powerful talons, flapped their massive wings, and flew backwards, yanking out entire sections of netting, large enough for them to fit through.

A thunderbird dove out of the Aviary and swooped down on the hotel roof, silencing the shrill horn as it ripped it off the post with its mighty talons.

The other thunderbird beat its wings and went all the way up and perched on a girder beam. It wasn't long before the giant bats and the other winged cryptids escaped, gliding and hovering in the tenebrous dome.

# 24

## LOCKDOWN

Sixteen of his men were already suited up in the gunroom when Ivan entered the armory. They wore black helmets with grilled face shields, puncture proof body armor vests in the event of a sharp-clawed animal attack, and tactical uniforms. Each member of the two-man teams was either armed with a short barrel, large magazine riot shotgun, a compact submachine gun, or a pneumatic tranquilizer rifle.

Everyone had Beretta nine-millimeter fully automatics holstered on their utility belts along with sheathed 8-inch long serrated combat knives, high-powered flashlights, stun grenades, and ammunition pouches.

"Okay, listen up," Ivan shouted to get everyone's attention like a football coach about to say a few words before sending his team out onto the playing field. "With the cameras down, we have no idea what's going on out there. Hopefully, none of these creatures have managed to escape. I need for you men to secure the habitats. If at all possible, use your tranquilizer guns, if not, kill the damn things." Ivan turned when he heard footsteps approaching the open doorway.

Jack Tremens rushed in with Miguel. "What's going on?"

"All we know at the moment is there's been a power outage and a possible breech in the zoo's containments," Ivan said.

"Don't tell me those animals have gotten out?"

"My men will resolve the situation. I'm sending a team over to the hotel. Think you and Miguel could go with them, make sure everyone stays inside? The last thing we need is for a bunch of hysterical people running around out there getting themselves killed. Here's a list of the guests." Ivan handed Jack a folded paper.

"Sure, let us grab our gear." Jack put the list in his pocket. He went to the locker where he and Miguel stored their equipment and weapons whenever they visited the dome. He took out their high-powered rifles and leaned them against the locker door.

"Looks like Carter Wilde's little petting zoo just turned into a frigging circus," Miguel said to Jack as they strapped on their sidearms.

Jack released the cylinder on his revolver, making sure it was fully loaded with cartridges, then snapped it closed. "And now it's time to send in the clowns."

\*\*\*

Cam rubbed the grit from his eyes as the dust settled in the tenebrous tunnel. He turned and gazed at Tilly sitting in the passenger seat. She was coughing so hard, tears had streaked her ash-covered face.

"You okay?" Cam asked.

"I think so," Tilly answered, still coughing. She made a crude noise in her throat, turned away from Cam and spat out a thick wad of phlegm. She reached in her pocket, took out a handkerchief, and blew her nose profusely.

The Cushman's headlights had dimmed so Cam could only see a short distance but it was enough to see fallen rubble was blocking the tunnel. "Doesn't look like we're getting out that way."

Cam slipped the gearshift into reverse to back up but when he pressed on the accelerator the cart didn't move. He fiddled with the key hoping that would work.

"The battery's dead," Tilly said. "We'll have to walk back, follow the side tunnel over to the lab."

"You sure you want to do that? What about the worms?"

"What choice do we have?"

"All right." Cam slid off his seat and raised the cushion. Inside were two flashlights and a large crescent wrench. He slipped the tool in the back pocket of his jeans and handed a flashlight to Tilly.

They headed back down the tunnel and soon reached the junction.

Cam panned his flashlight on the walls and ceiling before they continued on down the passage to the parking area that wrapped around the foundation under the lab and workshop.

A swath of light flashed across the wall.

Cam and Tilly turned. An electric cart with bright headlights was coming down the tunnel erratically, heading in their direction.

"Who is that?" Tilly asked, shielding her eyes from the glare with her hand and getting ready to jump out of the way.

"Must be that damn Beecher," Cam said unable to see the driver clearly.

The cart veered to the right suddenly and crashed into the wall.

Cam and Tilly started to rush over then stopped dead in their tracks.

There was definitely someone sitting behind the wheel in the cart because they could see the legs twitching. The rest of the person was inside what looked to be a giant sock puppet but in reality was a gluttonous Mongolian death worm gorging down its meal.

***

Nick was surprised to see other guests in the lobby demanding to know what the disturbance was outside the hotel even though the annoying siren had turned off.

He counted around fifteen, some of them still in their pajamas and robes, others looking like they had hastily thrown on some clothes. Everyone seemed to be talking at once. An irate man leaned on the front counter giving the hotel clerk a piece of his mind.

"What's with all the people?" Gabe asked.

"Jesus, Nick it's a damn mob," Meg said.

"Let's hang back, see if the manager or somebody shows that can tell us what's going on." Nick pointed to a loveseat and a chair on the far side of the lobby away from the fracas.

They stayed clear of the boisterous crowd and were almost to the sitting area when Nick heard shattering glass. He turned and saw a bili ape had smashed through a dining room window.

The primate knocked aside tables and upended chairs as it charged through the room, drawn to the noisy group of people. It moved with athletic agility, thrusting both arms out and landing on its knuckles, rump and bent hind legs tucking between its elbows with each bound.

"Oh my God," Meg yelled when another ape jumped through the empty window frame.

"Holy shit!" Gabe gasped.

Nick steered Meg and Gabe behind one of the giant palms. They crouched behind the massive ceramic pot and poked their heads up.

The two bili apes charged into the crowd like a couple of deranged lunatics causing everyone to scream and flee to get out of their way. The primates were relentlessly brutal, attacking one person then another, striking them down with their powerful fists, shattering bones and ripping off limbs.

Nick cringed when a blonde woman trying to get away was snatched by her long hair and with one swift jerk, her scalp was ripped from her skull.

He watched as a young boy was picked up and flung across the lobby floor, screaming, until he struck the wall.

When a man fell to the floor, his right leg was seized and yanked clear out of the socket, tearing off his pant leg, and showering the bili ape with spurting blood.

Nick couldn't believe the amount of blood pooled on the granite floor as the bodies continued to fall.

The agonizing cries soon died away as the last victim was silenced.

The massacre left dismembered corpses in the middle of the lobby; the front desk and surrounding walls covered with crimson splatter and gore.

The apes stood fully erect, raised their blood-drenched hands in the air and screeched, baring their red-stained teeth in a victorious display of savagery.

Nick ducked down and looked at Meg and Gabe. They were scared out of their minds. He wondered if they were even too frightened to move, especially after what they had just witnessed.

He glanced over his shoulder and spotted a fire door maybe twenty feet away. If they could reach it, they could run up the stairs and lock themselves in a room until help came. It was their only chance.

"We need to get out of here," Nick whispered to Meg.

"But where?" Meg asked.

Nick directed her and Gabe's attention to the fire door.

"But they'll see us."

Nick raised his head to take a peek at the apes and saw they were squatting in the middle of the pile of bodies, hunched over, relishing their first taste of human flesh.

"Dad?" Gabe whispered.

"What, son?"

"Weren't there four on the tour?"

Nick saw one of the apes raise its head and look directly at him. "We need to go! Now!" He grabbed Meg by the hand and yanked her to her feet. He pulled her along and ran as fast as he could for the fire door. He glanced back for a split second. Gabe was right on their heels.

And so was a giant ape, its face and chest caked with blood.

Nick reached the fire door and flipped down the handle. He pushed the door open enough for Meg and Gabe to slip through then followed them into the stairwell.

The bili ape flung its body against the other side of the door then shoved its face against the small eight by ten inch window, and snarled, leaving a blood smear on the glass.

"Hurry, up the stairs," Nick shouted.

Meg rushed up first, then Gabe.

Nick grabbed the banister and scampered up the stairs after them.

They had just reached the third floor landing when Nick heard a tremendous bang down below.

He stopped, leaned over the railing, and peered down.

The ape was clambering up the stairwell.

# 25

## CHAOS

As soon as they left the security building, Jack and Miguel followed the two-man team down the pathway to the front entrance of the hotel. The guard with the shotgun put up his hand upon reaching the glass door, signaling everyone to stop.

Jack could see bodies lying on the lobby floor.

"It's a damn slaughterfest in there," Miguel said.

The other guard caught Jack's attention and pointed to a bili ape pulling a long strand of tendon out of a dead person's arm with its teeth.

"I've got this," the guard with the tranquilizer gun said.

"No, wait," Jack objected but it was too late, the guard had already opened the door and charged in.

Eager to subdue the animal, the guard dashed across the floor. With the stock of the non-lethal air gun pressed against his shoulder, he took quick aim, and fired a projectile.

The dart struck the ape in the nape of the neck. There was enough immobilizing sedative in the hypodermic dispenser to bring down a horse.

The bili ape yanked the dart out of its fur just as the guard shot it again, hitting it between the shoulder blades.

"Get back you idiot!" Jack shouted, storming in after the guard.

The ape reached over its shoulder to extract the second dart but it couldn't quite reach it. It stood and turned around. Once it saw the guard rushing towards it, the infuriated ape roared and charged its assailant.

Before the guard knew what was happening, the ape grabbed the man's helmet by the grill and gave it a fierce shake.

Jack heard the guard's neck crack.

The ape held onto the helmet and dragged the limp body along the floor like a toddler would a rag doll.

Jack took a bead on the ape with his high-power rifle and fired a single shot.

The slug punched a hole in the ape's forehead just above its right eye and exited out the back of its skull in an explosive pink mist of fragmented bone and minced brain.

The ape toppled backward onto the pile of dead bodies.

"Nice shot," said the guard with the shotgun.

Jack turned on the guard. "Didn't anyone tell you guys that tranquilizer darts don't work on bili apes?"

The guard was taken aback and could see Jack was angry. "Miller got excited and must have forgotten," the guard replied in his defense.

"The last thing you want to do, is underestimate these creatures," Miguel said. "That is, if you want to stay alive."

"Miguel's right. You better pass the word to your boss. Make sure nobody else makes the same mistake."

"Yes, sir." The guard stepped away and got on his two-way radio to call his boss.

Jack looked around at the mutilated bodies. "What a goddamn mess."

"Don't these apes travel in troops?" Miguel said.

"They do."

"Then where're the rest of them?"

\*\*\*

Nick held the fire door open for Meg and Gabe as they rushed into the third floor hallway. He could hear the ape bounding up the stairwell a floor below.

He tried pulling on the door but the attached door closer over the jam wouldn't allow him to slam it shut. He backed away from the door and turned.

Meg and Gabe were working their way down, dodging into the small alcoves outside each suite, trying the doors to see if someone had propped one open.

"Hey, what the hell's going on?" yelled a baritone voice.

Nick saw a man standing outside one of the closed doors further down the hall.

"Thank God!" Nick yelled, "Let us inside your room."

"What for?"

"There's an ape coming up the stairs."

"A what?"

"AN APE!" Meg and Gabe yelled at him.

Just then the bili ape ripped the fire door off its hinges and stomped through the doorway.

"Jesus, you weren't kidding," the man yelled. He turned to his door and grabbed the handle. "Damn thing won't open. I'm locked out!"

"That's cause there's no power," Nick said. "They only open from the inside."

"So what the—"

The bili ape charged down the hall on all fours.

"Run!" Nick yelled at the man and took off down the hall after Meg and Gabe who were already running away.

Nick heard the man scream but didn't look back. The ape howled and then there was a loud crash of splintering wood, which probably meant the primate had flung the man through his suite door.

Some of the emergency lights had not activated, so the far hallway was extremely dark. Nick could just make out Meg and Gabe's silhouettes. He could hear the ape stampeding down the hall.

He felt a sudden pressure and cupped his hand over his forehead. It was like a wedge was being forced between his skull and the front of his brain.

And with it, came a vision.

*Don't go in!*

"Meg! Gabe! Wait!" He ran as fast as he could and reached his wife and son just as they were about to step between the opened doors of an elevator car. He grabbed them both by the arms, pulled them back, and pushed them aside to the carpet.

Nick spun around and hit the floor, just as the ape dove over him into the black void, smashing into the metal wall of the elevator shaft.

\*\*\*

Jack turned when he heard a muffled impact behind the closed doors of the lobby elevator. "What the hell was that?" he asked Miguel.

"I don't know."

They stepped around the bodies to the elevator. The guard pulled his combat knife from the sheath on his utility belt and used the tip to pry open the doors. Jack and Miguel each grabbed the edge of a door with their fingertips and together yanked them apart.

"Holy shit!" Jack said when he saw the crumpled body of the bili ape with its feet in the air inside the car, covered with ceiling tiles and debris. The ape was clearly dead having crashed through the roof and landing on its head.

The guard wasn't taking any chances after seeing his friend brutally killed and vindictively fired his shotgun, turning the ape's head into an unsavory bowl of crimson mush.

Jack stepped inside the car. He shined his flashlight up the elevator shaft and saw a man, woman, and a teenage boy staring down at him from three flights up.

"You okay up there?" he yelled.

"We are now," the man answered.

\*\*\*

Cam and Tilly were sickened by the sight of their coworker being swallowed alive by the Mongolian death worm and made their way around the circular foundation with their backs pressed against the wall, afraid they might be next.

"Did maintenance ever repair that hydraulic service elevator that connects between the lab and the workshop?" Cam asked.

"I'm not sure," Tilly said. "But even if they have, doesn't it run on electricity?"

"It has its own auxiliary power. For emergencies, like this."

"It's worth a look."

They continued to skirt around the foundation until they reached the wide elevator doors with a control box on the wall. Two dust-covered vehicles were parked in the small lot: a black sedan and a large moving van.

Cam opened the cover on the panel. "We're in luck. They must have fixed it because the auxiliary switch is on." He pushed the button to open the elevator doors and heard Tilly gasp.

"What's wrong?" he said and turned.

A tzuchinoko had crept up and was only ten feet away. The upper part of its body rose in the air. The Japanese snake looked like an obese cobra. It opened its mouth and hissed, baring its venomous fangs.

"Don't make any sudden moves," Tilly said.

"You mean like *run*?" Cam said, doing his best to remain calm. He glanced over his shoulder and saw that the doors had opened on the elevator.

"What do we do?"

Cam saw something moving out in the murky underground structure. "Step back into the elevator."

"Are you crazy? We'll be trapped."

"Trust me," Cam said and pulled the crescent wrench out of his back pocket. He waited until Tilly was in the elevator then slowly stepped in, never once taking his eyes off the snake's evil glare.

The snake tensed, ready to strike.

Cam struck the elevator door repeatedly with the end of the crescent wrench.

The clanging startled the snake momentarily.

Cam and Tilly stood apprehensively as the elevator doors slowly closed but then were quickly elated when a Mongolian death worm—drawn by the sound—loomed out of the darkness over the fat serpent and plunged downward, swallowing the snake.

# 26

## RAMPAGE

Ivan had no idea what to expect when he went outside and dispersed his security teams throughout the grounds. The interior of the dome was like being in a massive subterranean cavern illuminated by only a few torches—in this case sparse emergency lighting—forcing them to have to use their flashlights. He could just make out the silhouettes of some of the buildings in the near pitch black. So many shadows and dark niches for the creatures to hide and lay in wait.

He could hear mighty roars booming from Mammoth Arena on the opposite side of the dome. It was the enormous bear and the giant ground sloth. By the sound of things, the two were either having an altercation or were just pissed off from being cooped up.

They were not a priority as long as they remained in their enclosures, giving him more time to contend with the lesser threats.

He had assigned a two-man team to accompany him. All three of them were armed with Heckler & Koch MP7 submachine guns with 40-round clips, ample firepower to bring down any of the cryptids in the zoo.

They were somewhere near the laboratory and workshop complex when he heard what sounded like heavy wings flapping overhead. "Guns up!" he hollered and crouched down, aiming his weapon in the air.

Ivan heard a *whoosh* then a man screamed. He directed the beam of his flashlight and saw one of his security guards being hoisted in the air, his body clutched in the talons of a gigantic thunderbird. The man continued to scream and kicked his legs like a little kid having a tantrum.

"Do we fire?" yelled the other guard.

If they did, they might get lucky and hit the bird of prey but most likely the bullets would kill the guard first.

The giant bird soared straight up and was quickly beyond the reach of Ivan's flashlight. "Jesus, he's gone."

Ten seconds later, Ivan heard a wet splat on the flagstone path. He trained the beam on the source of the sound. It was the guard that had just been scooped up or so he believed.

"Son of a bitch," the one guard said when he saw the man's splattered body on the paving stones.

"It must have taken him all the way up to the top and dropped him," Ivan said, wondering why it would do such a thing. It was unbelievable the destruction a 25-story fall could do to a human body.

He heard someone yell not too far away. "Come on," Ivan said to the guard and they scurried down the pathway, following the beams of their flashlights.

Ivan saw another one of his teams standing near the gap between the lab and workshop complex and the Biped Habitat. The men were twenty feet apart with their backs turned, looking in opposite directions.

"What's going on?" Ivan asked.

"I saw a blue tiger," one of the men said. "It's over there!" He trained the muzzle of his shotgun at the side of the building.

"No, it's over here," shouted the other man, pointing his assault rifle in the other direction. "It doubled back around the building. Damn thing's stalking us."

Ivan and his guard stepped back not knowing which man to believe.

"There it is!" one man yelled. The other man turned and rushed over to his teammate.

Ivan gazed in the same direction but didn't see anything. He figured they were probably spooked and were seeing things. The last thing he needed was for his men to get trigger-happy and start shooting each other.

Suddenly, two blue tigers appeared out of the darkness and pounced on the two men from behind, pinning them to the ground with their long, sharp claws.

Ivan and the guard standing next to him hesitated, afraid if they fired, they'd hit the guards. But when Ivan heard the tigers cracking open the men's skulls with their powerful jaws, he knew they were already dead. "Take 'em down!"

Both Ivan and the guard opened up on the closest tiger, riddling its body with bullets and emptying their clips. Ivan was about to train his weapon on the other big cat when it ran off, dragging the dead guard by the head, and disappeared into the dark.

***

When Jack called up and told them to come down to the lobby, Nick, Meg, and Gabe rushed through the hallway and hurried down the stairwell.

When they stepped out through the fire door they saw the bodies and all the blood. Meg had gotten weak-kneed and would have collapsed on the floor if Nick hadn't caught her. Gabe's face had become ashen and he averted his eyes from looking directly at the mutilated guests.

Guiding them over to where they had been sitting before, Nick told Meg and Gabe to hang tight while he conferred with the others to see what was going on.

Jack watched Nick approach. Nick introduced himself, pointed to his family, and then they shook hands.

"I take it you're an employee?" Jack asked.

"That's right. Marketing. But you probably already know that."

"Not really. Do you have an idea how many of you came here?"

"Ah, I'd say, maybe ninety."

Jack glanced over at the bodies. "I'm going to need an exact headcount."

Nick saw two more security guards enter the lobby. One of them walked over to Jack. "Sir, Mr. Connors told us to check with you. See if we could assist."

Jack looked over at the guard with the shotgun standing near a door just off the front desk. "Hey, where does that lead?"

The guard opened the door and peeked inside. "Looks like a conference room," he hollered back.

Jack gave the guard a wave. "Thanks." He turned to the two men that had just arrived. "Let's do a quick clean up. Move the bodies into the conference room. And cover them with table cloths. See if you can drag a hose in here and wash away this blood before we start getting more people to come down."

"Yes, sir. Right away." The guards slung their weapons over their shoulders and got right to work. Miguel went along to give them a hand.

"Anything I can do?" Nick asked.

"Not unless you can identify some of these bodies and I can scratch them off my list," Jack said, producing a folded up piece of paper.

"No, but there's a boy upstairs I'd like to go up and get," Nick said.

"I'd prefer if you and your family stayed down here. That way I'll know you're safe. Don't worry, I'll make sure security gets him when they bring down the others."

"Sure, I understand." Nick tagged along and followed Jack as they took a roundabout way over to the front desk so they didn't have to step over bodies or tread in any blood.

They had just come around the backside of the counter when they saw the mutilated body of the poor hotel clerk lying on the floor. He remembered she'd been an attractive young woman.

After a few minutes, the guards had moved all of the bodies except for the hotel clerk's into the conference room.

Another guard came into the lobby and propped the double doors open that led out to the pool area. He dragged in a long hose and positioned himself so when he turned on the high-pressure nozzle, he was able to spray the blood in the direction of the opened doors.

Nick figured he'd hose the stream of blood outside and direct it down a drain.

While Jack went over the list, Nick returned to his family. He sat down on the couch between Meg and Gabe and put his arms around their shoulders. "Don't worry. They're working on a plan to get us all out of here."

"Thank God," Meg said, leaning against Nick.

Nick looked at Gabe. "Don't worry buddy, Jack assured me they'd find Shane."

Gabe stared down at his sneakers but didn't say anything.

\*\*\*

Cam and Tilly stepped out of the service elevator onto the main floor and headed down the dark passageway, using their flashlights to guide them.

"Let's check to see if anyone's in the lab," Tilly said.

"Yeah, maybe they know what's going on." Cam led the way. Soon they were at the long bank of windows outside the laboratory. He pressed his face close against the glass and gazed in. "It's too dark to really see...wait a minute. I think there's someone in there." He shined his flashlight but got too much reflection off the glass so he put it down by his side.

Tilly and Cam banged on the glass to get the person's attention.

"Where were they?" Tilly asked, cupping her hands beside her temples and looking in.

"I can't see them. Maybe it was just a shadow."

"Aren't there sleeping quarters in this building for people who work weird hours?"

"Yeah, for the lab and animatronics techs. I think Burt Owen and Professor Howard also have their own private rooms. I'll bet they're back there. We should go wake them up."

"Don't you think it's a little strange that no one's up? I mean, they must have at least felt or heard the explosion."

"We better go see." They turned right at the junction and followed the hallway down to a series of doors.

"This must be where most of them sleep," Cam said, reading the plaque on the door. "Should I knock?"

"Just take a peek."

Cam grabbed the doorknob and twisted. As soon as he cracked the door, he could smell the overpowering odor. "Jesus, there must be a gas leak." He opened the door all the way and held his nose as he entered the large room.

There were six military-style bunk beds lined up along the walls, each with a pale-faced person with blue lips, lying on a mattress.

Cam kept his nose and mouth covered and searched the room.

"Do you hear that?" Tilly said, her hand over her mouth.

It was a hissing sound, coming from behind a radiant heater by the wall. Cam approached and could feel his eyes begin to burn. He glanced behind the radiator and saw that the coupled line had come loose and was the source of the gas leak. Cam reached down and inserted the thin pipe back into the fitting. He took the crescent wrench out of his back pocket and tightened up the nut, stopping the gas from escaping. He shoved the tool back in his trouser pocket.

Tilly fanned the air with her hand, going from upper to lower bunk, checking for pulses or seeing if anyone was breathing. "Oh my God, Cam. They're all dead."

"Must have been caused by that damn explosion," Cam said.

"We better see if the professor and Mr. Owen are here," Tilly said.

They dashed out of the room and went down the hall to the next set of doors.

Not bothering to knock, Cam opened the door to Professor Nora Howard's room. She was lying on a single-size bed. A glass of water was on a nightstand, next to a vial of pills.

"Ah, shit!" Cam rushed to the bedside and shook the woman.

"What?" Nora said, groggily.

"Professor, are you okay?" Cam asked.

"Yes, but what are you doing in here?"

"Something horrible has happened," Tilly said, stepping into the room.

Nora sat up. She was dressed in a rumpled blouse and a pair of wrinkled slacks. She swung her feet onto the floor. "What is it? What's wrong?"

"The lab techs and Mr. Owen's crew are dead."

"What do you mean, dead?" Nora asked, slipping her feet into her flats.

"They were asphyxiated by a gas leak in their room."

"Oh God," Nora said.

"Didn't you hear the explosion?" Cam asked.

"What explosion?"

"It took out the main power grid."

"I took some sleeping pills and must have been so zonked out, I didn't hear it."

"Is Mr. Owen here?"

"I believe so."

"Then we better see if he's okay," Cam said. They rushed out of the professor's room and down the hall.

Before they reached Burt Owen's door, they could hear him yelling inside his room.

"Mr. Owen, can you hear me?" Cam shouted.

"Yes. Who's out there?"

"Cam Morgan. I'm out here with Professor Howard and Tilly O'Brien."

"My door's stuck, I can't get out," Burt shouted from the other side.

"Hold on, let me try from this side." Cam tried opening the door but it was as if the doorframe had shifted, wedging in the door. He spotted a glass cabinet with a fire ax inside. He went over, took out his crescent wrench, smashed out the glass, and pocketed his trusty tool.

He reached in and took out the ax.

"Okay, everyone, stand back." Cam waited until Tilly and the professor were clear and swung the ax blade at the door, chopping out the entire locking mechanism.

Burt opened the door. "Thank you, young man. We better see to the others."

Cam and Tilly exchanged looks then turned to Nora.

"What's going on?" Burt asked.

"I'm sorry, Burt, they're all dead," Nora said. "My people and yours."

"But how?" Burt said in disbelief.

But before anyone could tell him, a menacing roar sounded from down the hall.

"What the hell was that?" Burt said.

"I don't know, but I think it's coming this way," Nora said.

"Quick, we can hide in the workshop."

Everyone followed Burt down the hallway. He opened the door and stepped into the animatronics assembly area. "Get behind those workbenches."

Before they could get situated, a tall figure appeared in the doorway.

Burt took one look and yelled, "It's the damn yeti."

Entering the large room, the abominable snow creature roared and flung out its right arm, smashing the head off a clay lizard sculpture on a table.

"I guess that's not one of yours," Nora called out from behind the workbench.

"Unfortunately, no," Burt replied, grabbing a control box wired to the incomplete bigfoot covered with fur except for its metallic arms and legs.

The yeti spotted Burt and stomped across the room.

Burt held the controller in one hand and operated the toggle switch with the other.

Before the yeti could get at Burt, the motorized bigfoot came to life and blocked its path with its heavy body. The snow creature slammed its fist into the bigfoot's face but its mechanical opponent wasn't fazed.

Burt did a fancy maneuver and got the bigfoot to sidestep the yeti. The bigfoot's metallic arm swung upward like a guillotine between the yeti's arm and body. The sharp edged metal sliced up the armpit, cutting through bone, and severed the limb at the shoulder.

The yeti roared with pain as blood spurted out the gaping wound. It stared down at the blood-soaked appendage lying on the floor by its feet and bent to pick it up.

Burt set his creation into motion and cranked up its speed.

The bigfoot collided head-on with the yeti, the impenetrable steel head caving in the bio-engineered cranium. The yeti crashed to the floor.

Burt turned off the control box and the animatronic bigfoot froze in mid-motion.

"Jesus," Burt said, gazing down at the dead yeti. "How the hell did that get out?"

"We think the zoo's been compromised," Tilly said.

"Yeah, they're escaping everywhere," Cam piped in.

"Oh my God," Nora said. "I have to get over to the Biped Habitat."

"Sorry, professor, but I don't think that's a good idea," Cam said.

"I agree," Burt added.

But Nora wasn't listening to reason and started for the door.

Cam ran after her and grabbed her by the arm. "Seriously, Professor. You don't want to go out there."

Nora stopped and looked at Cam's hand on her arm then gazed up at him. "You don't understand. If what you've said is true, and all the creatures are running loose, that means Connors' men are out there right now hunting them down. I can't let that happen."

"But how are you going to stop them?"

"I don't know but I have to try."

"But those things are dangerous."

"Not the yeren. It wouldn't hurt a fly. I can't stand by and watch them kill it. You stay here if you like but I'm going."

"No, I'm going with you," Tilly said.

"Okay, I'm coming too." Cam looked at Burt Owen.

"You three go. I'll see if I can find help. Maybe I can get word to Connors. Good luck to you."

"Thanks, Burt." Nora dashed out, followed by Cam and Tilly.

# 27

## PANDEMONIUM

Nick stood with Meg and Gabe in the lobby and waited while the security guards canvassed the hotel and checked each suite on every floor and brought the guests down the stairs in small groups. So far, they had rounded up around fifty people as they continued their search. Apparently, some had managed to sleep through the disturbance while others had been apprehensive to leave their rooms.

Luckily, the dead bodies had been removed and the cleanup was completed before the first arrivals had showed up. Nick imagined their horrified faces if they could have seen the fancy lobby looking like an abattoir.

A dozen more people filed out the fire door into the lobby. When it seemed the last person had come out, Nick said, "Still no Shane."

"Don't tell me he took something and is out cold," Meg said. She looked at Gabe accusingly.

"Mom, I already told you. He wasn't feeling well." Gabe shifted his eyes to the floor.

"Is there something you're not telling us?" Nick asked.

Gabe continued to stare at his sneakers.

"Gabe!"

The teenager looked up at Nick. "It's not my fault."

"What's not your fault?" Meg asked.

"It was Shane's idea, not mine."

"Let's hear it," Nick said.

But before Gabe could answer, another group of guests started piling out of the stairwell.

Nick raised his hand. "Wait, let's see if he's with these folks."

A woman screamed from the other side of the lobby.

"What the hell!" a man yelled.

Soon other people were shouting and screaming.

"Oh my God, Nick!" Meg pointed into the dining room.

Winged creatures were flying in through the busted out window, entering the hotel like a bizarre air raid.

A giant bat swooped into the lobby, snatched a little boy by the scruff of his shirt, and to his mother's horror, flew off with him. Five more ahools soared in and dove into the crowd, flapping their enormous wings over everyone's head.

Nick turned when he heard a scream and saw a flying snake attacking a woman; its thin skinned wings wrapped around her face as it sank its fangs into the top of her skull. Two more arabhars glided in over everyone's heads. The venomous serpents latched onto guests trying to flee and clung onto their backs.

Jack and Miguel ran in from outside through the propped open lobby doors and saw the panicked crowd running in every direction. They pointed their rifles trying to get a bead on the flying creatures but they couldn't shoot for fear of hitting someone.

Nick moved his family against the wall near a hallway entrance that led to the suites on the ground floor.

Two ahools broke away from the melee and flew at them.

"This way!" Nick yelled, motioning for Meg and Gabe to run down the hall.

The farther they went, the darker the passageway became as all of the emergency lights were out except for the last one at the very end of the hall.

Nick spotted a walking cane on the carpet that someone had dropped and left behind. He bent down as he ran and scooped up the cane. He could hear the giant bats' wings flapping behind him as they steadily closed the gap.

"Dad, there's nowhere for us to go," Gabe shouted as he and Meg reached the end of the hall by an alcove for the ice machine.

Nick swung the cane and shattered the emergency light.

The passageway went pitch black.

"Down on the floor!" Nick yelled.

The giant bats flew right over them and crashed into the wall with a sickening crunch. Their heavy, lifeless bodies thudded on the floor.

Nick stood up in the dark. He could see the light at the other end of the hall leading into the lobby.

"Nick, how'd you know they'd crash into the wall?" Meg asked. "Did you have another one of your visions?"

"No. Weren't you paying attention during the tour?"

"Oh, yeah, right. Christine said ahools couldn't navigate in the dark."

"Bingo!"

Nick could hear gunshots and more people screaming but it seemed to be further away. "We better see what's going on now."

They sprinted down the hall and stepped warily into the lobby.

Jack spun around, aimed his revolver and shot a giant bat before it could attack a woman huddled on the floor protecting her child. The bullet punched a gaping hole through the ahool's chest. It hung in the air for a brief moment like a kite caught in an updraft then plummeted to the floor.

Miguel stood in the middle of the lobby. He held his big pistol in a two-handed grip and was taking careful aim, picking off one giant bat then another.

One of the security guards was bashing a flying snake into the marble floor with the butt stock of his rifle.

Most of the people were running through the open doorway leading out toward the pool area.

"We better follow them," Nick said.

Jack and Miguel dashed for the doorway to join them.

They had only gone maybe twenty feet outside when they heard everyone scream and come running back.

Nick couldn't believe his eyes.

People were being lifted into the air by gigantic suction cupped arms coming out of the pool. A man was smashed against the hotel wall while another was dragged down into the water.

Nick counted six arms flailing about, grabbing one person after the other as they tried to run past.

"Holy shit!" Miguel said. "How'd the kraken get in the pool?"

Jack got as close as possible and fired into the water.

"How about we try these?"

They all turned and saw the head of security, Ivan Connors. He was holding a stun grenade in each hand. He pulled the pins and lobbed them into the water. Two bright flashes of light appeared under the crystal clear water followed by twin concussions that sent a pair of geysers spewing up out of the pool.

Nick gazed down at the deep end of the black bottom pool and saw a shape forming as the giant octopus' camouflage changed to its natural pigmentation.

The kraken's head came to the surface.

Jack and Miguel fired their handguns while Connors strafed the giant octopus with his machinegun. Bodies bobbed to the surface as black ink clouded the water.

The rest of the kraken floated up and looked like a giant deflated balloon from a Thanksgiving Day Parade.

"My God, Nick," Meg said. "Is Carter Wilde out of his mind? Why would he even create such a place?"

Nick shook his head. "Maybe he meant for it to be a *scream* park."

"You guys okay?" Jack asked, looking at Nick and his family.

"We're still alive if that's what you mean," Nick smiled sheepishly.

Jack glanced over at Miguel. "Gather everyone up and head for the main entrance."

"Aren't you coming?" Miguel asked.

"I have to find Nora. Make sure she's okay." Jack turned and took off into the dark.

Meg looked at Nick. "See, I told you they were an item."

# 28

## LAB RAT

Dr. McCabe had spent an hour preparing the backroom in the laboratory for surgery. He wore lime-green surgical scrubs, nitrile gloves, and a blue mask over his nose that covered some of his beard.

Two battery-operated camping lanterns were set up on each side of the operating table so as not to cast shadows over his work. A cart was next to the operating table and was filled with surgical tools, each item laid out in the proper order of usage, as he didn't have anyone assisting him during the procedure and didn't want to be distracted groping around for the correct implement, none of which were sterilized.

As the door leading into the lab had a window, he'd covered the glass with black plastic to block out the light so no one would know he was back there.

He gazed down at his patient.

The pregnant chupacabra was semi-unconscious from a mild sedative and was lying on her back on the small operating table. Both of her arms were at right angles like she was being crucified and were strapped down on arm boards with tight Velcro. Her feet were slightly spread apart and were bound by the ankles to the end of the table.

Her protruding belly looked like a ripe watermelon. The taut skin would bulge in places as the babies moved about inside her womb.

Dr. McCabe grabbed a scalpel from the cart and made his first incision down the mid-line section of the mother's abdomen. Blood started to seep out of the thin wound exposing a layer of yellow fat and the fibrous fascia over the stomach muscles. He made another incision, cutting through the layer from the upper abdomen to the pubic bone, and set the scalpel on a towel.

He used a pair of scissors to further open the cavity then pressed the tissue apart with his gloved fingers. He continued to use the scissors and snipped through the peritoneum, the next layer covering the bowel.

Normally he'd be extra careful so as not to nick the bladder, causing an infection but he wasn't concerned about the patient's well-being and time was of the essence so he just delved into the next stage.

He took the same scalpel and made another incision then used a retractor to widen the opening. He pushed away the bladder, exposing the uterus and counted three babies.

Stepping on a foot pedal under the operating table, he turned on the suction pump and used a hose to remove most of the blood covering the babies to prevent them from drowning in their mother's fluids. He shoved in some sponges to soak up more of the blood.

He took each baby out, snipped the umbilical cords, and clamped the bellybutton nubs. He cleaned them up with a towel and placed them in a large incubator on a wheeled cart.

They were as ugly as their mother—maybe even more so—and made creepy little mewing sounds.

He removed his mask and scrubs and tossed them on the floor. Backing across the room and pulling the incubator cart, he opened the adjacent soundproof door with his hip.

The cacophony of sounds was like walking into a jungle teeming with wildlife and got even louder as he came inside the cryptid nursery. He pulled the cart all the way into the room and let the door close.

Many of the cages had been removed from their shelves and niches and were stacked on pushcarts ready to be transported in the event of an evacuation.

A baby bigfoot stared out through its tiny bars.

Thunderbird chicks hopped about on their perches. A red-eyed mothman peered out from its gloomy cage. A couple of ahools hung upside down with their wings wrapped around their small bodies.

A black mngwa kitten and a blue tiger kitten were curled up in the back of their cage next to a Bergman's bear cub.

A Buru flicked out its thin tongue and hissed from its cage as the other reptilian cryptids moved about in their separate glass terrariums.

Two miniature-sized sauropods stood in an open crate.

Inside a sealed Plexiglas cube resided a mysterious gelatin glob.

The other bioengineered infants watched the doctor with mild curiosity.

Dr. McCabe looked down at the incubator and was surprised to see the three baby chupacabras roll over onto their bellies, push themselves up into standing positions then press their tiny two-fingered hands against the glass and begin to bawl.

Their cries were so loud Dr. McCabe had to cover his ears.

"Shut up!" he screamed. When he took his hands away, he was shocked to discover that all the creatures in the nursery had gone quiet except for the keening chupacabras.

Unable to take it anymore, Dr. McCabe grabbed the handle and opened the soundproof door into his impromptu surgical theater.

The mother chupacabra was wide awake, her head raised off the operating table with a horrified look her on her hideous face, gawking at the gaping hole in her abdomen and shrieking as she fought fretfully to free herself from her restraints.

# 29

## LENNIE

If Jack didn't know any better, he would have sworn he was running through a battlefield with all the random gunfire and the distant screams. He had his rifle slung over his shoulder across his back as he found it easier to run armed with his Colt .45 magnum revolver.

He caught a glimpse of a gun muzzle flash to his left and silhouettes of people running madly through the grounds.

Somewhere in the darkness an animal yowled, most likely one of the big cats.

High overhead, a loud squawk echoed in the cavernous dome.

He reached the main entrance to the laboratory and animatronics workshop complex and went in slowly. He crept down the tenebrous hallway past the windows facing into the lab, his gun cocked and ready. The obscure room was dark and it didn't appear like anyone was inside. He tried the door and found it to be locked.

Further down the corridor, he saw movement beyond an open door.

"Anyone there?" he called out, not knowing if it were a person hiding in the room or a creature waiting to jump out at him.

"Who's asking?" answered a voice.

"Jack Tremens!"

"Hey, Jack! It's Burt."

Jack rushed over just as the special effects wizard appeared in the doorway of the workshop. "It's like a war zone out there."

"Tell me about it." Burt motioned to the dead yeti lying on the floor in a puddle of blood next to its severed arm.

"You did that?" Jack asked.

"You might say I had some help," Burt replied with a grin.

"None the less, you might want to stay inside until we get a better handle on things."

"You didn't by any chance see the professor and those two zookeepers?" Burt asked.

"No. I came over thinking Nora was here."

"They went over to the Biped Habitat."

"What? Doesn't she know these animals have gone berserk?"

"She was worried about the yeren."

"I think that big ape can take care of itself."

"Apparently, she thinks differently."

"All right. Once I find them, we'll swing back for you."

"Okay, Jack. You be careful."

Jack dashed down the hallway. He went out the side exit door and followed the path leading over to the other building.

Before entering, he took a moment to listen for any animal sounds. When he didn't hear anything, he walked through the open doorway and went inside.

The first thing he noticed was the putrid smell. He switched on his flashlight and shone the beam down the hall.

There were brown splats on the floor: bili ape crap.

He stepped around the smeared piles and continued down the hall to the observation area.

As he hadn't heard any noise, he thought he'd take a chance and make his presence known. "Anyone in here?" he yelled out.

Jack placed the flashlight alongside the barrel of his gun and slowly turned around in a circle. He didn't see any activity until his light shone into the yeti habitat and he saw one of the creatures crouched in front of the snow cave. Even though the bright light was shining directly into its eyes, it didn't look away. When it didn't react, Jack knew it had to be the animatronic and wasn't a threat as it was programmed to remain where it was.

He panned the light to the yeren habitat. The door was wide open and something was moving behind the big ferns. He kept his gun pointed straight ahead and shined the beam on the dense vegetation.

"Jack?" a woman's voice said from behind a giant frond.

"Nora. What are you doing back there?"

"We're hiding with the big fella. You better get in here quick!"

Jack lowered his gun. He shined the flashlight on the floor and was about to step into the enclosure when he heard scampering feet behind him. He spun around and shined the light into the hall.

Four chupacabras screeched and recoiled from the bright light.

Jack switched off the flashlight then turned it back on, catching a fleeting glimpse of the goatsuckers scampering out the main entrance and disappearing into the dark.

"It's okay, they're gone."

"Are you sure?" Nora asked, poking her head out from behind the large leaf.

"Trust me, they're gone."

Nora came out of the bushes and was followed by two zookeepers that Jack knew only by their first names, Cam and Tilly.

"Where's your boyfriend?" Jack asked. He'd often kidded Nora that she spent way too much time with the timid 12-foot tall ape-man, which bonded to her like an endearing pet. The creature reminded Jack of the John Steinbeck character, Lennie Small in the novella *Of Mice and Men*.

Nora turned and whistled softly like a chirping bird.

The giant ape-man stomped out of the brush, knocking over a fake tree with a swing of its arm.

Jack always thought the Chinese wildman looked like an orangutan wearing a baseball umpire's chest protector and had the misfortune of being sent to the dungeon and stretched on a torture rack.

He was about to make a wisecrack when Nora pointed over his shoulder and screamed, "Oh my God, Jack, I thought you scared them off?"

"I did." Jack turned and was surprised to see a bigfoot standing in the open doorway. The eight-foot tall sasquatch snarled and stormed into the enclosure.

Jack fired one shot then another.

The first bullet struck the hairy creature in the shoulder, causing it to falter and clamp a beefy hand over the wound. Then the second slug creased the bigfoot's cheekbone, shearing off a patch of its face. Blood flowed out of the gash and poured down its neck.

Jack hoped it would be enough to make it turn and run but he was wrong.

The beast hunched its shoulders in a hostile stance and glared at Jack.

"I'll stay and hold it off while you run out the back," Jack said, glancing over at Nora and the two zookeepers.

"We might get trapped," Tilly said. "The rear doors aren't working properly."

"She's right. We were going to report it but never got the chance," Cam said.

Jack took a step back. Cam and Tilly were to the right of Nora who was standing directly in front of the tall ape-man.

The yeren stared at the savage creature standing only fifteen feet away but didn't show any signs of aggression. Jack feared the good-natured ape-man was too passive to realize the potential danger it was really in.

Again, the Chinese wild man reminded Jack so much of the man-child, Lennie from Steinbeck's story.

The bigfoot charged.

Jack aimed for the center of its chest and pulled the trigger. The hammer came down with a disturbing click. He'd been in such a hurry rushing over to find Nora that he had neglected to reload after leaving the hotel.

He dropped the big revolver.

Reaching back, he grabbed the butt stock of his rifle slung over his back, and swung the barrel up, sticking his finger into the trigger guard...

The bigfoot struck Jack such a powerful blow he was knocked off his feet and sent flying back into the jungle foliage. Hitting the ground, he felt like a mule had kicked him. He gasped for air hoping the bigfoot hadn't broken his ribs.

"Hey, get back!" Cam yelled. He had grabbed a tree branch and was swinging it back and forth trying to scare the bigfoot. Tilly was standing next to Cam, wielding a long stick at the beast, which at the moment seemed more interested in Nora. It was as though it understood that the woman was responsible for its deployable existence being locked up and now had a way of seeking revenge.

Jack started to reach for his rifle but a sharp pain in his side made him wince. He gazed around and saw his revolver almost within reach only five feet away, but still useless without bullets.

When Cam and Tilly moved to protect Jack, the bigfoot lunged at them. It backhanded Cam across the face, sending him sprawling to the ground. Then it swung its other arm, cuffing Tilly on the side of the head and sending her into the bushes.

The sasquatch growled and went for Nora.

Nora screamed and crossed her arms in front of her chest to fend off its attack.

The yeren grabbed Nora by the shoulder with its enormous hand and pulled her back out of the path of the charging beast. The Chinese ape-man raised its right fist and came down like a sledgehammer directly on top of the bigfoot's head, cracking its skull.

Before the humanoid had time to fall, the yeren grabbed the 600-pound sasquatch by the arm, spun it around, and flung the creature through the glass partition. Glass shards exploded everywhere and hailed down on the floor on top of the bigfoot.

Though it was severely wounded, the bigfoot still attempted to get up.

Jack had just sat up when he heard rapid gunfire.

The bigfoot jerked and twitched as each bullet punched into its body before falling flat on its face.

A security guard dashed down the hallway, ejecting the clip from his assault rifle and slapping in a new one. "Professor Howard, move out of the way." He raised his weapon and aimed at the yeren.

"No, stop!" Nora screamed, raising her hands in the air and stepping in front of the giant ape-man.

"We've got our orders to kill these creatures on sight."

"Over your dead body," Jack said. He was on his feet but struggling with his rifle.

"I have my orders." The guard aimed at the towering yeren.

"Don't shoot, please don't shoot," Nora pleaded.

"Screw your orders. I'm telling you to..." but Jack never finished his sentence because the man was suddenly attacked from behind by a giant mngwa and slammed to the floor. The black leopard raked its claws into the man's back and bit out the back of his head.

The big cat turned and dragged the dead man off down the hall toward the exterior door.

"Jesus, that thing just came out of nowhere," Cam said.

"Is anyone hurt?" Jack asked, taking shallow breaths.

Nora looked at Tilly and Cam. "You guys took quite a wallop."

"Just a few little bruises," Tilly said and turned to Cam. "Right?"

"Yeah, but that bigfoot would have killed us for sure if it weren't for the yeren," Cam said rubbing his shoulder.

"Looks like we owe Lennie a debt of gratitude," Jack said.

"Lennie?" Nora asked.

"Don't you think it's about time you gave your boyfriend a name?"

Nora looked up at the Chinese ape-man. "What do you think? Should we call you Lennie?"

The 12-foot tall yeren looked down, stuck the tip of its tongue out between its black lips, and made everyone laugh when it blew Nora a raspberry.

# 30

## SMACKDOWN

When Ivan spotted the headlights of two golf carts rolling down the flagstone pathway toward Mammoth Arena, he yelled to the guard accompanying him to hustle and they started jogging to the back of the dome.

They were almost there when Ivan heard a thunderous crack and saw a five-foot thick section of concrete as big as a billboard sign topple out of the massive enclosure wall. Tons of rubble landed directly on top of the men in the golf carts, crushing them and flattening the vehicles.

"Son of a bitch!" Ivan yelled.

Two humongous shapes appeared in the opening.

The giant ground sloth stumbled out, its massive claws making it difficult for the five-ton prehistoric-era beast to clamber over the chunks of cement.

Bergman's bear was right behind the clumsy creature, swiping its flank with its sharp claws.

The larger animal bellowed and turned. It stood up on its hind legs to confront its attacker using its thick tail as a tripod to balance itself.

The bear rose up to its full height of sixteen feet and faced the taller elephant-sized Megatherium. It let out a beastly roar and stomped up to the other creature. Each animal swung at the other, slashing through fur and creating monstrously deep wounds.

Ivan watched as the two embraced in a wrestling hold, each one attempting to overpower the other with pure brute strength.

The bear opened its mouth, bit into the sloth's neck, and tore out a chunk of flesh the size of a mattress, creating an enormous wound gushing blood like a ruptured fire hydrant.

Weakened by the massive loss of blood, the sloth stepped back. Its tail slipped out from under it and the mammoth creature fell backward.

Ivan felt the tremble under his boots as the sloth hit the ground.

The bear got on top of its fallen adversary. It mauled the other beast with its teeth and claws and didn't stop until the giant ground sloth ceased moving and was dead.

"Now's as good a time as any," Ivan said. He readied his assault rifle and ran toward the bear, which at the moment was ripping through the belly section of its victim.

The security guard was right beside him and aimed his weapon.

"Fire!" Ivan squeezed the trigger and unleashed a quick burst of bullets. It was difficult to tell in the dark but he believed many of them hit some part of the bear by the way it reacted and yowled with pain.

The man next to him had emptied his clip and was grappling for a fresh magazine from his belt.

That's when the bear retaliated and charged.

Ivan was surprised a 4000-pound bear could move so fast and yelled, "Run!" to the other man but by then it was too late.

Having fired off every round in his clip and no time to reload, there was nothing Ivan could do to save the man, who was dead with one swipe of the bear's powerful paw.

Ivan bolted down the pathway.

Bergman's bear lumbered after him.

Veering off the flagstone path, Ivan dashed across the artificial turf and up the hill, hoping the bear would be exhausted from battling the giant ground sloth.

But the bear didn't show any signs of slowing down. On the contrary, it seemed drawn by a new scent as it bounded up the hill.

Ivan reached the top and dashed by the Sea Monster Cove sign. He looked over his shoulder and saw the bear come up over the crest.

With nowhere else to go, Ivan headed down the bleachers. He jumped from one row down to the next, praying he didn't trip and fall.

He heard a loud roar.

Then the aluminum bleachers shook as the bear lumbered down.

Ivan was almost to the bottom when he realized if he was to escape the bear it meant diving into the cove and possibly jumping into the open jaws of the cadborosurus.

He didn't know what would be worse: being savagely eaten by a bear or swallowed up by a sea serpent.

Then the bear made the decision for him.

Ivan heard a thunderous crash and looked up. The bear was tumbling down the bleachers. Ivan frantically tried to get out of its way. He scooted under the bench seat just as the bear bounced over him and crashed down into the water.

Ivan stood and watched the bear swim over to the beach. He could also see the shape of the sea serpent cruising underwater around the other side of the small island.

A mokele-mbemebe ambled out of the cave.

The bear shook its wet coat and advanced on the small brontosaurus. It rose on its hind legs, took a couple of awkward steps, and came down on the sauropod's back, biting into its slim neck. The bear shook its head in an attempt to tear away the flesh but its teeth seemed to be caught on something.

Finally, after a frantic struggle, it was able to pull free.

Ivan could see blood dripping out of the bear's mouth. He quickly realized the blood wasn't the sauropod's when he saw the metal glinting from the animatronic's ravaged neck. The sharp edges must have cut into the bear's gums and tongue causing them to bleed.

Enraged, the bear backhanded the sauropod, knocking it over onto its side. The legs moved robotically in the sand for a moment then went still.

Taking the opportunity to reload his weapon, Ivan dug out a fresh clip from his ammo belt.

He ejected the empty magazine and was about to insert the new one when the giant sea serpent raised its head out of the water. He watched breathlessly as the enormous creature swung its long neck over the sand and clamped its sharp teeth on the nape of the bear's neck, but when it tried to drag the two-ton carnivore into the water, the bear reached up and clawed at the sea serpent's face, its sharp nails raking the thick skin and gouging out an eye.

The cadborosaurus let out a pitiful wail, released the bear, and dove back down into the murky water.

Ivan couldn't believe what he had just seen.

It was like something out of a science fiction movie.

The giant bear charged across the sandy beach and up the steep slope on the opposite shore, tearing out enormous chunks of turf as it climbed to the top.

Ivan slapped in a new magazine and ran back up the bleachers.

Reaching the crest, he saw the giant bear smash its way through the front doors of the aquarium and enter the building. He bolted down the hill hoping he might trap the animal and prevent any further destruction.

When he reached the front entrance, he could hear the bear bellowing inside. Ivan stepped over the broken glass and twisted metal and headed down the dark hall. He edged around a corner with his weapon ready.

Bergman's bear was salivating, standing on its hind legs, facing the glass front of the aquarium as it watched the magnificent selection of fish swimming around the coral reef centerpiece. Thick drool hung from the corner of its mouth.

Ivan had the perfect shot.

He raised his sub machinegun and pulled the trigger—at the same instance the bear caught his scent and spun around—and only grazed the bear's shoulder, forty rounds pummeling the glass.

Ivan watched in horror as spider cracks spread wildly from the indentations made by the bullets. He turned and ran for his life as the giant bear roared and the thick glass of the 900,000-gallon aquarium burst apart like a rupturing dam.

# 31

## MASS EXODUS

Nick, Meg, and Gabe gathered with the remaining thirty people clustered in the hotel lobby while Miguel took a moment to speak with the two security guards that had stayed behind to help round everyone up.

Nick did a quick sweep of the faces around him then turned to Meg. "I still don't see Shane. You don't think he ran out with the others?"

"If he did, the poor boy is probably dead," Meg whispered so Gabe wouldn't hear.

"Jesus, what are we going to tell Bob and Rhonda? We were supposed to be watching out for him."

"How do we know Bob even survived the heart attack?"

"Aren't you little Miss Doom and Gloom," Nick said.

"I think under the circumstances..."

"We can't stay here," Miguel shouted. "Our only chance of survival is finding a way out of the dome and getting to the buses."

"That's suicide," a man in a bloody shirt said.

"We'll never make it," a woman joined in.

"Has anyone had any firearm training?" Miguel asked.

Most of the adults in the group shook their heads.

Nick raised his hand. "I've been to the range." He'd gone with Bob when his friend had first purchased a handgun for home protection and talked Nick into tagging along. Between them, they had fired nearly fifty rounds but then the gunpowder had gummed up the cylinder to the point that it wouldn't close up so they were forced to call it a day. Nick never went again. For all he knew, that same gun was still sitting in Bob's nightstand and had never been cleaned.

Miguel turned to one of the security guards. "Karl, let him have your Glock and give him some pointers." Miguel looked at Nick. "Remember, safety on at all times unless you have to fire."

Karl handed Nick the pistol and explained how to operate the weapon.

"Please be careful," Meg said once the condensed training was over. She draped an arm around Gabe's shoulder.

Nick could tell his son was withdrawn and was going into shock.

"Don't worry, Gabe. We're going to get out of this place," Nick promised, holding the handgun down by his side.

"We should head for the main entrance," Miguel said. "I want everyone to stay together. Whatever you do, don't fall behind."

Everyone nodded complacently.

Miguel and the two security guards went out first, followed by the group of employees and their families and hustled down the wide pathway.

They hadn't traveled more than fifty feet when Nick heard a tremendous rumble and saw a torrential surge of floodwater rushing down at them.

Everyone was swept off their feet by the fast moving two-foot high deluge.

Nick grabbed Meg who was holding onto Gabe's hand. As he tried to pull them up he saw hundreds of silver fish floating by, thrashing in the fast-moving water. A sand shark brushed against him with its rough skin and left an abrasion on his forearm.

He had to push Meg out of the way of a large bluefin tuna flopping past.

Nick heard a woman scream and turned just in time to see a tiger shark slide into her and clamp its jaws around her legs, dragging her with it through the rushing water.

The floodwater became shallower as it spread about the dome, the sodden grounds teeming with floundering fish that looked as though they had washed up on a beach after a tsunami.

"My God, Nick," Meg said, on her feet and completely drenched. "What caused the Tank to burst?"

But before Nick could answer, a humongous shape bounded over the swampy grounds, splashing its way between the two rows of cryptid statues, its wide girth brushing against the towering sculptures, toppling some of them over to crash down like felled trees.

It was Bergman's bear leaving a path of destruction in its wake.

The bear smashed through the main entrance gate allowing a portal of natural sunlight to filter in.

"Everyone, follow me!" Miguel yelled, sloshing toward the main pathway.

A gust of wind blew into the dome, ripping the tarpaulins off the statues of the spine-chilling monsters that still remained on their pedestals.

They had only passed the first set of statues when Miguel raised his arm and everyone came to an abrupt halt.

"Oh my God!" a woman yelled.

Nick saw a fifteen-foot Buru with something dangling out of its mouth, step out from behind a pedestal. He spotted another monitor lizard, creeping across the mushy ground, swishing its tail.

A terrible smell permeated the air.

Nick put his hand over his nose and mouth. He counted six corpses with huge bite wounds on various parts of their bodies, lying near the flagstone path. Their flesh was slowly rotting from the bacteria left on their skin by the Burus' saliva.

"Good God, Nick. Is that Christine, our tour guide?" Meg gasped, pointing to the dead woman in the polo shirt, raw patches of skin sloughing off her arms.

Nick couldn't swear to it, but he was pretty sure it was.

Miguel and the security guards directed everyone to sidestep past the deteriorating corpses.

Suddenly a man screamed from the group.

Nick turned around and saw what appeared to be a red spear protruding out the man's chest. Then he saw the wings spread open and realized it was a long-beaked kongamato that had impaled the man; only it wasn't strong enough to lift its speared prey off the ground.

He knew he couldn't do anything to save the man but he could prevent the giant bird from attacking someone else. He walked up, thumbed off the safety, and shot the cryptid in the head. Its wings folded and it slumped to the ground next to the dead man.

"Look out!" another man yelled.

Nick turned and saw a giant thunderbird swoop down and snatch the man up in its talons and airlift him over the main pathway and out the gaping hole at the main entrance.

Miguel and another security guard fired their guns as more cryptids appeared out of the gloom, stampeding their way to freedom.

Nick grabbed Meg and Gabe and they ducked as two giant bats flew right over their heads followed by other winged creatures.

"Hurry!" Miguel shouted.

The brute strength of Bergman's bear was evident when they finally reached the main gate, which had been smashed apart like a bulldozer had driven through.

Nick shielded his eyes from the bright sunlight as they ran out. It was so good to finally be out of the dome.

"Over here!" a voice called out.

It was the driver, Sam Kerry, standing next to his black charter bus, waving everyone over.

The group—Nick counted maybe fifteen people excluding Meg and Gabe that had survived—funneled into the opened door of the bus.

He saw Miguel and the two security guards run back into the dome.

Nick was one of the last ones about to board. He heard footsteps behind him and turned.

A man with a blood-smeared shirt was hobbling toward Nick with his arms outstretched. "Help me," he begged.

But before Nick could do anything, a giant Mongolian death worm burst out of the ground and pulled the man back into its hole.

Nick froze, like his feet were trapped in ice.

"Nick!" Meg yelled from the bottom of the bus steps. "Get in here!"

The big diesel engine started up with a rumbling roar.

Nick snapped out of it, turned...

Only to be confronted by a giant bili ape. It stood ten feet away and was blocking his way to the bus. The four hundred pound chimpanzee screeched, displaying its pink gums and vicious teeth.

Nick brought the Glock up to arm's length and commenced firing, keeping his finger twitching on the trigger, one round after the other, watching as the powerful slugs punched holes in the giant lion-eating chimp's chest.

The burly primate staggered and fell to the ground.

Sam was steering the bus in a wide turn.

Nick ran up and jumped inside as the door closed behind him.

He glanced through Sam's side window and caught a glimpse of the dome's blue roof as they drove through the trees.

Meg and Gabe were sitting together in the front seat behind Sam.

Nick sat in the seat across the aisle. He gazed over at Gabe who had his head rested on Meg's shoulder. His son looked catatonic.

"My God, Nick," Meg said, tears in her eyes. "Look what that place did to our boy. He's a mess. We're going to sue that bastard for everything he has."

But Nick knew this wasn't the time to tell her that suing Carter Wilde was never going to happen as he and every other employee of Wilde Enterprises that had been chosen to bring their families to Cryptid Zoo had signed a waiver of liability agreement.

He reached across the aisle and took Meg's hand.

"Let's be thankful we made it out of there alive and worry about that                                                         later."

# 32

## DISAPPEARING ACT

Jack stood by while Nora beckoned the yeren to follow her. She'd been concerned for its safety and thought it best that it stayed inside the building. As a large section of glass was missing from its own habitat, she coaxed the Chinese ape-man into the bigfoot's enclosure as it had a natural setting with trees and ferns and wasn't that much different to the jungle that it was accustomed to.

Cam and Tilly gathered up bundles of fruit and brought them over so the yeren would have something to eat. The big ape sat on the floor with bunches of bananas on its lap. It stripped off a banana and shoved it into its mouth, skin and all, and slowly mashed it into pulp with its enormous teeth.

Confident that the big ape would adapt to its new surroundings, Nora backed out of the enclosure and pushed the door closed.

"You know you can't lock it in," Cam said.

"I know," Nora replied. "But as long as it's content, it won't have any reason to leave the habitat. Isn't that right, Lennie?"

The yeren grunted and pushed another banana between its lips.

"Unbelievable. I think it knows its name," Tilly said.

"I promised Burt Owen that I'd come back for him," Jack said.

Nora looked away from the yeren and faced Jack. "Then we'll need to swing by the lab."

"Why? I don't think any of your staff are in there."

"You don't know?" Cam said to Jack.

"Know what?"

"The lab technicians and Burt's crew are all dead."

"What? But how?"

"A gas leak. We think it was caused by the explosion in the tunnel."

"We were down there when it happened," Tilly said.

"My God," Jack said and looked at Nora. "I'm so sorry."

"Which is why we need to get to the lab." Nora walked off and headed down the corridor to the exit door.

Jack, Cam, and Tilly rushed after her.

When they stepped outside, everyone was surprised to find everywhere sopping wet.

"What the hell, did we have a flood?" Cam said.

They ran across the boggy ground and entered the next building.

Jack turned on his flashlight and shined the beam down the hallway.

Burt Owen stepped into the light. "So, you made it back."

"Told you I would," Jack replied.

Jack heard footsteps coming from the other direction. He looked over his shoulder and saw Miguel running towards him, carrying his own flashlight.

"It's a frigging zoo out there," Miguel said, stopping to catch his breath.

"Well, yeah, we all know that," Jack replied with a grin.

"No, I mean it's insane. Bergman's bear destroyed the aquarium."

"That explains all the water."

"It also busted out of the dome. These things are running loose everywhere."

"You mean they've gotten out?"

"That's what I'm saying."

"Holy shit," Jack said. He turned and saw Nora rushing toward the laboratory. "Hey, wait up!"

Nora had her access card out and was trying to swipe the lock but it wouldn't disengage.

"You better stand back and let me open it," Miguel said.

Jack pulled Nora away from the door.

Miguel drew his Desert Eagle .357 magnum and fired one shot, blowing apart the locking mechanism. He kicked in the door.

Nora rushed in and scurried past the workstations to the back of the room, Jack and the others close behind.

When she opened the door to the nursery, Jack knew something was wrong right away even without looking inside.

It was absolute quiet.

"Oh my God," Nora screamed. "They're all gone."

Jack stepped into the threshold and panned his flashlight all around the room. The shelves were all bare, every cage and terrarium gone.

"I'll be right back," Miguel said and dashed back through the laboratory.

Jack thought he heard something and pushed open an adjacent door.

"Ah, Jesus," he said. Nora stepped beside him as Cam, Tilly, and Burt crowded around to see what had evoked such a strong reaction from Jack.

They stared at the whimpering chupacabra with the gaping hole in its abdomen, strapped to the operating table, victim of a botched abortion. It tried to raise its head then fell back, heaving its last breath.

"The bastard," Nora growled. "He did this."

"You mean Dr. McCabe?" Jack asked.

"Who else." Nora stormed out and went over to another door. She opened the door and waited for Jack to come over to provide some light. Cam, Tilly, and Burt gathered around the doorway so they could see inside the room.

Jack shined the flashlight around the small office. A workbag with yellow and orange stripes was on the desk.

"Hey, that looks like the bag that maintenance guy had, the one that was working on that electrical panel," Cam said, poking his head through the door.

Jack stepped up to the edge of the desk. He unzipped the bag and looked inside.

"There're some tools. Christ, there's a block of C4 and some fuses."

"You mean Dr. McCabe blew up the power grid? But why?" Cam asked.

"Most likely for a diversion."

"So he could steal the babies," Nora said.

"But why?" Jack asked.

"To get back at Carter Wilde. McCabe figured as he had bioengineered these creatures they were rightfully his and wanted to get a patent for all of his creations. Only Wilde refused. He figured if he was footing the bill, they were his property and legally his."

"You don't think the doctor had anything to do with that gas leak?" Burt asked.

"He probably figured it was the best way to make sure no one would be around to mess up his plans."

"Son of a bitch."

Jack heard Miguel call out his name. "We're over here!" he yelled, stepping out of the office.

Miguel came back through the laboratory and stopped. "He must have used the freight elevator. It's on auxiliary power and wasn't affected by the outage. Also, the moving van in the garage is gone."

"Well, now we know how he got them out of here," Jack said. "So where did he take them?"

"I know how we can find them," Nora said.

# 33

## HOME AT LAST

It had only been 18 hours since Nick and Meg had brought their son home and already every radio and television station was abuzz about strange sightings of bizarre creatures which after an aerial search led authorities to the Cryptid Zoo dome. Nick figured they must have locked the place down once they saw all the bodies.

Every time Nick flipped through the channels, there would be a field reporter standing in the woods outside the blue, beetle-shaped stadium relaying what limited information was made available as now the theme park was under federal investigation and was completely sealed off from the public.

There'd been strange sightings populating social media. A cattle rancher claimed a bear as big as a house attacked one of his herds and carried off one of his prize bulls in its mouth. Two campers swore they had seen a bigfoot and posted actual pictures of the creature. A road crew arrived to what was believed a sinkhole that had collapsed a patch of pavement and saw a giant worm burrowing in the earth. The escaped cryptids were becoming an overnight sensation as more incredible accounts bombarded the Internet.

Nick had ignored the phone knowing it might be someone from his work trying to get him to agree to some bullshit story so as to cover the company's ass. He'd seen investigative reporters trying to get a statement from Carter Wilde but he refused to comment. Nick wouldn't have been a bit surprised if he had already skipped the country knowing all the lawsuits that would surely come raining down on the billionaire's head from relatives of those brutally killed.

He knew it would only be a matter of time before the press learned about his family and their nightmarish vacation. The last thing they needed right now was for a bunch of reporters to be banging on their door. His poor son had retreated to his bedroom the moment they had stepped into the house, and hadn't come out since. How many hours of therapy would it take to erase the things he'd seen?

Nick wanted to get in contact with Bob and Rhonda but hadn't a clue as to where they were or who could give him that information. It was almost as though Bob and Rhonda Pascale had disappeared off the face of the planet. He still wasn't sure what he would say if they asked about Shane. For now, it was best to just wait and see what happened.

He'd showered and changed his clothes and wanted to lie down and rest but knew he couldn't sleep for fear of what might wake him up in the night. Which was why he was sitting at the kitchen table at three in the morning, nursing a bottle of Michelob Ultra Light.

Soft footsteps entered the kitchen.

"You, too, huh?" Nick said as he watched Meg reach into the refrigerator and come out with her own bottle of beer. She twisted off the cap and took a swig before sitting down across from Nick.

"So, what now?" Meg asked, placing the bottle on the table.

"Might be a good time to dust off my resumé, what do you think?"

"You don't think there'll be a settlement?"

"What, to hush us up? You'd be willing to take it?"

"If it would make our boy well. Have you called your mom to tell her we're home?"

"Not yet," Nick said. "You know what we forgot?"

"What?"

"Raise your bottle."

Meg picked up her beer and held it out.

Nick clinked the glass neck of his bottle with Meg's bottle.

"Happy anniversary."

* * *

"That's him," Nora said to one of the FBI agents standing with her by the departure gate checkout counter. The tall agent that reminded her of Vince Vaughn stepped in front of the bearded man wearing a plaid flannel shirt and dungarees.

"Dr. Joel McCabe?" the agent asked.

"Uh, yes," McCabe hesitated.

"You are under arrest for murder and the possession of stolen goods."

McCabe glanced over the FBI agent's shoulder and saw Nora. "You? How did you find me?"

"It just so happens you made the mistake of traveling at the same airport."

"What do you mean, the same airport?"

"Jack and Miguel and the FBI are down on the tarmac right now, seizing your shipment for the Ukraine."

"I don't know what you're talking about."

"Sure, you do," Nora said. "What, were you planning on selling them to the highest bidder?"

"Sure, why not? I certainly wasn't going to hand them over to that selfish bastard Wilde."

"Looks like you both lose."

"You still didn't tell me how you found me?" McCabe said as the FBI agent pulled the doctor's hands behind his back and slipped on the cuffs.

"By following your trail."

"What trail?"

"The one left by the cryptids," Nora said. "I'm sorry, maybe I should have told you."

"Told me what?" McCabe asked as the agent started to march him away.

"That I implanted GPS tracking chips inside each of the babies."

# 34

## FINAL SWEEP

FBI Special Agent Mark Jennings had been to more crime scenes than he cared to count but had never seen so many dead bodies in one place as this one. Forensics eventually gave up trying to cordon off each victim with yellow tape and decided to treat the entire indoor zoo as one big crime scene. The Army Corp of Engineers had been called to restore power so the lights were back on.

Jennings' assignment was to go door to door in the hotel with the guest list and do a thorough check of each suite. He had two agents with him that were instructed to gather and catalog the residents' belongings for the investigation, which would be returned if the people were still alive.

Each time he opened a door, the men would brace themselves in the event a creature was lurking inside. So far they had found nothing.

"Any chance we could take a break and grab a bite to eat?" one of the lower grade agents asked Jennings.

"Sure, after we check this next room." Jennings used the master keycard and slid it in the door lock. He waited for the light to go green, lowered the handle, and then pushed the door open.

Once all three of them were in the room, the agent that was anxious to take a break said, "Doesn't look like anyone was even in here."

Jennings looked at the guest list. "That's odd. Says here that a Bob and Rhonda Pascale were registered to this suite." He looked around.

The bed was made. There was even a mint on one of the pillows.

He glanced in the bathroom.

There were freshly laundered towels on the racks.

The countertop was spotless with neatly wrapped bars of soap and plastic drinking cups covered with thin, clear plastic.

Just the way the housekeeping maid had left it.

"Well, I guess we can..." but then he paused when he spotted a notation on the guest registrar. "Seems there's an adjoining room."

"Is that it?" one of the agents said, pointing to a door next to the dresser.

"Must be. Says here is it was reserved for their son, Shane, and another boy by the name of Gabe Wells. We better take a look."

The second Jennings opened the door he knew something wasn't right.

"Jesus, what's that smell?" gasped an agent.

"Something's dead in there," said the other, repressing the urge to gag.

Jennings covered his nose and stepped into the room. He felt along the wall with his other hand until he found the switch and turned on the light.

He looked across the room and saw two beds, one half-made with the sheet partially pulled down, the other bed covered with a bulky blanket, bulging in the center.

Jennings drew his sidearm and slowly approached the bed.

The room reeked like a catch that had been left out in the sun too long on the deck of a fishing trawler.

He could see the comforter was completely soaked—not from a liquid—but with a thick, translucent slime.

He reached down, grabbed a corner of the blanket, and slowly pulled it away.

The grotesque gray blob gazed up at Jennings with its two black eyes and pursed its repugnant mouth. It dragged itself a couple inches over the stained mattress with its two tiny arms.

"Good God, what is that thing?" one of the agents gasped.

"I have no idea," Jennings said, backing out of the room. "We better leave it for forensics."

Jennings turned off the wall switch and the room went dark. He stepped into the other suite and was about to close the adjoining door when he thought he heard...

*Please...Mister...helppp...meeee...*

He paused for a second then shook his head. "No, that's crazy," and shut the door.

# THE END

## ACKNOWLEDGEMENTS

I would like to thank Gary Lucas, Nichola Meaburn for her keen eye, and the wonderful people working with Severed Press that helped with this book. It's truly amazing how folks we may never meet and who live in the most incredible places in the world can truly enrich our lives. And I would especially like to thank my daughter and faithful beta reader, Genene Griffiths Ortiz, for making this so much fun and sharing these bizarre and incredible journeys.

## ABOUT THE AUTHOR

**Gerry Griffiths** lives in San Jose, California, with his family and their five rescue dogs and a cat. He is a Horror Writers Association member and has over thirty published short stories in various anthologies and magazines, and a short story collection entitled *Creatures.* He is also the author of *Silurid, The Beasts of Stoneclad Mountain, Down From Beast Mountain* and *Terror Mountain* as well as the Frank Travis and Rafferty family adventures *Death Crawlers* and their follow-up standalone novels, *Deep in the Jungle, The Next World,* and *Battleground Earth,* all published by Severed Press.

# CHECK OUT OTHER GREAT
# HORROR NOVELS

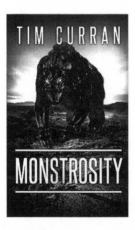

## MONSTROSITY
## by Tim Curran

The Food. It seeped from the ground, a living, gushing, teratogenic nightmare. It contaminated anything that ate it, causing nature to run wild with horrible mutations, creating massive monstrosities that roam the land destroying towns and cities, feeding on livestock and human beings and one another. Now Frank Bowman, an ordinary farmer with no military skills, must get his children to safety. And that will mean a trip through the contaminated zone of monsters, madmen, and The Food itself. Only a fool would attempt it. Or a man with a mission.

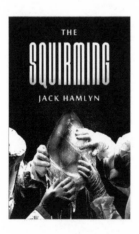

## THE SQUIRMING
## by Jack Hamlyn

You are their hosts.

You are their food.

The parasites came out of nowhere, squirming horrors that enslaved the human race. They turned the population into mindless pack animals, psychotic cannibalistic hordes whose only purpose was to feed them.

Now with the human race teetering at the edge of extinction, extermination teams are fighting back, killing off the parasites and their voracious hosts. Taking them out one by one in violent, bloody encounters.

The future of mankind is at stake.

And time is running out.

## CHECK OUT OTHER GREAT HORROR NOVELS

### DEATH CRAWLERS
by Gerry Griffiths

Worldwide, there are thought to be 8,000 species of centipede, of which, only 3,000 have been scientifically recorded. The venom of Scolopendra gigantea—the largest of the arthropod genus found in the Amazon rainforest—is so potent that it is fatal to small animals and toxic to humans. But when a cargo plane departs the Amazon region and crashes inside a national park in the United States, much larger and deadlier creatures escape the wreckage to roam wild, reproducing at an astounding rate. Entomologist, Frank Travis solicits small town sheriff Wanda Rafferty's help and together they investigate the crash site. But as a rash of gruesome deaths befalls the townsfolk of Prospect, Frank and Wanda will soon discover how vicious and cunning these new breed of predators can be. Meanwhile, Jake and Nora Carver, and another backpacking couple, are venturing up into the mountainous terrain of the park. If only they knew their fun-filled weekend is about to become a living nightmare.

### THE PULLER
by Michael Hodges

Matt Kearns has two choices: fight or hide. The creature in the orchard took the rest. Three days ago, he arrived at his favorite place in the world, a remote shack in Michigan's Upper Peninsula. The plan was to mourn his father's death and figure out his life. Now he's fighting for it. An invisible creature has him trapped. Every time Matt tries to flee, he's dragged backwards by an unseen force. Alone and with no hope of rescue, Matt must escape the Puller's reach. But how do you free yourself from something you cannot see?

## CHECK OUT OTHER GREAT
## HORROR NOVELS

### BLACK FRIDAY
### by Michael Hodges

Jared the Kleptomaniac, Chike the unemployed IT guy, Patricia the shopaholic, and Jeff the meth dealer are trapped inside a Chicago supermall on Black Friday. Bridgefield Mall empties during a fire alarm, and most of the shoppers drive off into a strange mist surrounding the mall parking lot. They never return. Chike and his group try calling friends and family, but their smart phones won't work, not even Twitter. As the mist creeps closer, the mall lights flicker and surge. Bulbs shatter and spray glass into the air. Unsettling noises are heard from within the mist, as the meth dealer becomes unhinged and hunts the group within the mall. Cornered by the mist, and hunted from within, Chike and the survivors must fight for their lives while solving the mystery of what happened to Bridgefield Mall. Sometimes, a good sale just isn't worth it.

### GRIMWEAVE
### by Tim Curran

In the deepest, darkest jungles of Indochina, an ancient evil is waiting in a forgotten, primeval valley. It is patient, monstrous, and bloodthirsty. Perfectly adapted to its hot, steaming environment, it strikes silent and stealthy, it chosen prey: human. Now Michael Spiers, a Marine sniper, the only survivor of a previous encounter with the beast, is going after it again. Against his better judgement, he is made part of a Marine Force Recon team that will hunt it down and destroy it.

The hunters are about to become the hunted.

Made in the USA
Middletown, DE
15 September 2018